Loving Bella

RENEE RYAN

Steeple
Hill®

Published by Steeple Hill Books™

STEEPLE HILL BOOKS

Steeple
Hill®

Recycling programs
for this product may
not exist in your area.

ISBN-13: 978-0-373-82836-4

LOVING BELLA

www.SteepleHill.com

Printed in U.S.A.

Brethren, I count not myself to have apprehended: but this one thing I do, forgetting those things which are behind, and reaching forth unto those things which are before.

—*Philippians* 3:13

To my father, Dr. Augustus Emmet Anderson, Jr.
This one's for you, Daddy!

Prologue

Theatre Royal, Drury Lane, London, England, 1885

Isabella O'Toole's life swept from one tragedy to another. And she loved every dramatic, heart-wrenching moment. Singing opera, as her mother once said, was in her blood. No matter the setting or situation, Bella always wept for her doomed heroines.

Tonight, however, there was an added layer of emotion that had nothing to do with tragedy. The sensation left Bella with a dull headache and unusually raw emotions.

He was here. In the audience. Watching her—*only her*—with the intense stare that never failed to steal her breath away.

The moment the curtain made its final descent her first impulse was to run to her dressing room and prepare for his visit. But that would be self-indulgent, a trait she disliked in others and thoroughly despised in herself. Somehow, she found the patience to offer congratulations to her fellow cast members with a genuine smile on her lips.

Still, in the back of her mind she was well-aware that he beckoned and there was little time left to prepare. She offered a quick hug to her understudy, and began the brief journey to her dressing room. Much to her amusement, she caught herself nearly running by the time she arrived at her destination. So much for dignity and grace under pressure.

With an impatient shove, Bella shut the door behind her and leaned against the sturdy wood. Thoughts of William filled her mind. Her heart pounded, her hands shook.

Conflicting emotions tangled inside one another, threatening to overwhelm her. Despite the joy of seeing William again, she was still on edge after playing Isolde. No matter how many times Bella sang the shifting chords in the final aria, the music rent every bit of emotion from her. She was exhausted.

Trying to force calm into her thinking, she breathed in and out. Tonight was too special, too important to allow grief for a fictional heroine's lost love to engulf her.

At last, the drumming in her heart shifted and she looked around the room.

Her refuge.

The one place solely hers, where she morphed herself from Bella O'Toole, youngest in the famous O'Toole acting family, into the most acclaimed opera singer of her day. With grace and comfort in mind, she'd decorated her small space by paying close attention to details and fuss. Intricate lace, fresh flowers and soft, cushiony furniture created a tone that was warm, feminine and fashionable.

To add a touch of glamour, Bella only used candles, preferring the soft golden glow and warm scent of the wax to the bleak ambiance provided by modern gas lamps. Perhaps she did have her moments of self-indulgence. But she tried to contain them to these small facets of her life instead of giving rein to the wild emotions that sometimes seized her.

Pushing from the door, Bella ran her finger along the edges of her makeup table, across the rims of the various jars of creams and rouge. Tools of her trade. Where she donned the mask of her characters and became the tragic heroines only found in the opera.

She spun in a circle and let dreams fill her head. Dreams of what life would be like if William proposed to her at last. Unlike the characters she portrayed, her love story would have a happy ending.

The charming, handsome viscount had been persistent in his pursuit of her over these last two months, often pushing for favors they both knew she would not give him until their wedding night. She was afraid, afraid he would come to mean more to her than she could handle. Afraid she would forget her moral upbringing and allow emotion to overpower her good sense. He already drew feelings out of her that no one else had.

In truth, his polished sophistication troubled her. Although she'd been raised in the theater, traveling with her famous parents and talented siblings across continents, she wasn't as worldly as Lord Crawley. Her parents had sheltered her from the uglier side of their profession. Reginald and Patience O'Toole had raised their children with Christian values and a strong knowledge of Scripture.

Bella often felt much younger than her twenty-four years. She missed her family. Especially now, when she desperately needed someone to talk to about her handsome viscount. Her mother or brother, Beau, would know what words to use to settle her unease, or rather what Scripture.

Oh, Lord, she prayed, *guide me.*

Whatever happens, conduct yourselves in a manner worthy of the gospel of Christ. Then, I will know you stand firm....

The words from Paul to the Philippians gave her confidence. Changing out of her costume would give her more. Bella bit back a sigh. With unsteady fingers, she quickly shed Isolde's medieval costume and changed into the dress she'd worn to the theater. The locket William had given her hung beneath the lace collar, warming her skin and reminding Bella of the viscount's deep affection, a tangible symbol of his love for her.

Sighing, she removed her stage makeup and laced up her boots. There was nothing left to do but wait.

As if on cue, the expected knock came at the door.

In spite of her efforts to remain calm and mature, a jittery surge of excitement tickled the base of her spine and she fingered the locket. "Enter," she said on a breathy whisper.

The door swung open. Bella's pulse drummed in her ears as her gaze connected with the man she loved. William Gordon. Lord Crawley. As she drank in the sight of her viscount immaculately dressed in black tails, she tried to look past the title and straight to the man.

He was tall and lean, his face aristocratic with a strong cut of cheekbones under deep-set blue eyes. Even the stark white of his shirt set off his dark good looks.

An unhurried smile drifted along his lips and he reached out his hand to her. Her pulse tripped, slowed to a near stop then quickened again. Tossing her head back, she started toward him.

He shut the door with a jab of his elbow and then lifted a single eyebrow at her.

Alone. They were all alone. Her stomach rolled over itself, but Bella continued forward. The click of her heels echoed across the parquet floor.

William was so appealing she wanted to rush her steps. She restrained herself. A moment like this required confident, liquid grace.

Tenderness and genuine appreciation mingled in his gaze before he covered his reaction with an unreadable expression. Her heart leapt to her throat and stuck. William Gordon was always kind, generous, quick-witted and charming. The sort of man a woman waited all her life to find. But he was also a man filled with hidden depths. And staring at her now, with such intensity, she realized he had a suggestion of danger about him.

With that thought, her steps slowed. She stopped a foot away from him and placed her palm in his.

"My beautiful, talented Bella," he said, lifting her hand to his lips. "You were magnificent this evening."

A jolt of impatience whipped through her at his standard compliment, but Bella hid the emotion behind a dazzling smile. Pleasantries first, sincerity later. That was their pattern. "Thank you, William."

He stared at her for a long moment, saying nothing. Seconds ticked by with only the sound of their breathing filling the barren silence. Bella's lack of experience with men made her unsure how to fill the awkward moment.

Searching for a clue as to how to proceed, she stared into his handsome face. A sudden gust of wind threw open the window behind her, blowing out the candles closest to her. Shadows filled half the room, concealing William's face. She thought she saw a flicker of something different in his eyes, something a little dark. A little unsettling.

A shiver iced across her skin and she felt the first stirrings of concern. Drawing her bottom lip between her teeth, she wheeled around, shut the window and quickly relit the candles. As she moved through the room, she reminded herself that this was her William. She knew him well. The realization settled her nerves.

"Where would you like to dine this evening?" His gaze shifted to the divan as he strolled toward her. "Or would you prefer to stay in?"

Bella looked around her dressing room. She eyed the soft lighting, breathed in the scent of a spring garden, noted the many pillows strewn on the divan. From a certain perspective one might mistakenly believe she'd prepared for something…illicit.

"I think we should go out," she said, flashing him a bright smile. "Celebrate my magnificent performance."

She'd hoped to make him laugh but his face remained impassive, and his shoulders stiffened. He drew her close to him and took both her hands in his.

"Tonight could be very special for us, my dear."

The sleepy charm in his manner pulled her a step closer.

He tightened his fingers around hers and commanded her gaze. "A beginning, if you will."

In spite of his pleasant tone, Bella couldn't shake the notion that something strange was creeping into their conversation, something sordid. She withdrew one hand and then another. "I—"

"Let us drop these pretenses at last." He shoved shaking fingers through his hair and started pacing along the edge of the Venetian rug. "You are too good for the theater."

He took her elbow and steered her to the divan.

Unsure of his motives, she slid away from him and perched against her dressing table instead.

"I have always dreamed of more," she said, her voice sounding as tentative as she felt. Where was this leading?

He opened his mouth to speak, then clamped his jaw shut as though he was considering his next words carefully. His breath came out in a ragged sigh. She feared his next words would define their fate and she wasn't sure she wanted to know the outcome.

At last, he nodded as if he'd come to some decision, rubbed his hand across his mouth and resumed his pacing. "It's good you want something other than the theater."

The satisfaction that shone in his eyes was at odds

with the tenseness in his movements. She'd never seen him quite so edgy. "William?"

"Let me provide for you properly," he blurted while never missing a step. "In the style and comfort you deserve."

His words staggered her and she found she had to clutch the side of her makeup table to steady herself. "Are you asking for my hand?" she asked, but she feared she already knew the answer.

He stopped pacing, turned to look at her with a frown marring his brow. "Marriage? You thought I came to offer marriage?"

His voice held genuine shock, as though the notion had never crossed his mind. She had to fight a wave of hysteria as she stared at him.

"You said you loved me," she said at last, touching the hidden locket with her fingertip.

He rushed to her, knelt at her feet and clasped her hands in his again. "I do love you, Bella." His breathing came in hard, shallow spurts. "It is why I offer my protection. It is the greatest gift I have to give."

He was no longer the suave viscount, but a man too desperate to have his way to remember his rank. The thought brought her no comfort, no hope. Only anguish.

She pressed her lips together to keep from sobbing and closed her eyes. Her heart pounded in her ears. "You think that little of me, of us, that you would make me your mistress?"

He squeezed her hands gently. "Look at me," he coaxed with his low, soothing baritone back in place.

She didn't think she had the courage, yet she forced open her eyes. The sincerity in his returning gaze gave her hope.

She held her breath.

"You deserve better than marriage, my love. I would never relegate you to the role of wife. It's nothing more than a gilded cage."

She lowered her eyes and said nothing, knowing no response was necessary. Very carefully, very slowly, she pulled her hands from his and straightened. He stood, as well.

"As an opera singer, I am not good enough to become your wife." She tilted her head to stare at him. "Is that what you are saying, William?"

"I love you too much to imprison you." He rose to his full height and continued. "As my mistress, you would have certain freedoms my wife could never have. I would give you a notice of carte blanche. You will never again incur a debt and will live a life of complete luxury."

The haughty tone of his words conflicted with the desperation she saw in his gaze. He looked so young, staring at her with those startling blue eyes. So sincere. As though he'd just offered her the most precious gift in the world.

"Yet, you don't love me enough to marry me."

He clasped his hands behind his back and drew in a long breath. "I already have a wife."

Bella gasped and her hand clutched at her throat. Her fingers brushed the locket which now weighed heavy around her neck. Chills swept across her skin, followed by scorching heat. Unable to speak, she stumbled backward until her spine hit the door leading to freedom. She dropped her gaze to her toes. From the hallway, a beam of light shone like a beacon under the door. She wanted to run from the ramifications she could not yet face, but that would make her a coward. Thus, she found the courage to demand further explanation. "You've pursued me all these months, while already married?"

"What I am offering is far more than marriage." He stood tall, head erect. His stance was full of aristocratic pride but his gaze held a silent plea. "Think of it, Bella, you will be the celebrated mistress of a viscount in his own right."

How could he think he offered her something of value, when it meant the desecration of his wedding vows? These long months of pursuit she'd held him at arm's length, had remained pure, all the while assuming he respected her as very few men respected women in her profession.

She'd been woefully mistaken. He hadn't been courting a wife. He'd been seducing a mistress.

She had just enough pride left to be furious at him. "I would like you to leave now."

Rage and anguish, guilt and love tangled in his gaze. "Bella, no, don't make a hasty decision. I love you."

His eyes begged her to believe him, and to her shame, she wanted to do just that. Hadn't she felt his admiration, respect and love grow deeper these past weeks? Was this how Bathsheba had felt when King David had pursued her? Was David's love so real and desperate, his arguments so convincing that Bathsheba willingly walked into sin with him?

Bella had never felt pity for the woman who committed such a brazen act of adultery. Until now. Heaven help her, Bella still loved William.

But the emotion shamed her.

Perhaps if she found the strength to walk away she could redeem them both. "I cannot accept your offer, William."

"I will not lose you, Bella. You are my greatest desire, I will die without you. I know I can make you happy. You will never want for anything."

Desire? Want? Was that how he defined love? She kept her head lowered to hide the spark of anger. At him. At herself for feeling such sorrow over her loss.

Marriage was sacred. *Therefore, what God has joined together, let no man put asunder.*

"I will not turn into an adulterer this night."

But she knew, in her heart, the deed was already done. Hadn't Jesus said that the thought alone made her accountable for the sin?

Apparently unaware of her turmoil, William turned his back to her, idly fiddled with the wax on a candle.

"I have pursued you these two months, have I not, with the benefit of nothing more than your smiles?" He sent her a shrewd glance over his shoulder, shifted to face her. "I honored your purity when I could have had any number of mistresses by now. I want you, Bella. The way a man wants a woman."

With each word he spoke, her disgrace grew. The room was suddenly hot, so hot she feared she would faint.

Dry eyes were her only defense. "I cannot become your mistress. I will not."

A range of emotions crossed his face again, more subtle and harder to read. The eyes that locked with hers were sharp and measuring. She knew he was calculating how best to win her. A wager he'd already lost. Bella would not harm an innocent woman.

At that thought, her mind was suddenly clearer. So clear it hurt. The churning in her stomach was humiliation, she knew. But she would survive.

Unfortunately, shame was a bitter taste on her tongue, one she feared would never go away. It helped to remind herself that she was not the victim here. Lord Crawley's wife bore that burden alone.

"Bella," he pleaded.

Their stares locked, held. He was so handsome. And she loved him so much. Even now. Still. Self-directed anger and misery bubbled up, but Bella forced it back with a hard swallow. She had to come up with a plan to get him to leave before she agreed to do something she already knew she'd regret. It was her only hope of salvation. "I need time."

A flicker of hope pulled his lips into a soft smile. "I understand." He drew her hand to his lips. "But make your decision quickly. I have been patient long enough."

It was a caddish remark, but Bella saw genuine emotion in the flash of anxiety that wavered in his eyes. In that moment, Bella realized he loved her. Truly loved her.

Yet, he would never understand her. His upbringing had taught him duty and possession and broken vows. Hers had taught her the sacredness of marriage and loyalty and obedience to Christ, her Lord and Savior.

With that last thought, her humiliation burned deeper. She knew what she had to do now.

It was only years of training that enabled her to look him in the eyes without breaking into tears, knowing this was the end. "Allow me one day to consider."

He dropped her hand. A smile hinting at his confidence slithered across his lips. "I will return before noon tomorrow."

She nodded. "Tomorrow, then."

A knot twisted in her stomach as she watched him walk out the door. There would be no additional meeting. Her only chance was escape. And she knew just the place to run, a place where William would never dare to follow.

A small victory, to be sure, but hardly an honorable one.

She could only hope with distance and time, absolution would come.

Chapter One

One month later, Denver, Colorado

He couldn't let her leave. Not without a fight. The spasm of panic shocked him, even as it pounded angry and insistent through his blood. For a moment—just one—Dr. Shane Bartlett had to fight the horrible urge to give in and beg, but he knew any display of emotion would be his doom.

For the sake of his patients, he had to ignore the choking sense of dread rising inside him and continue.

Jaw tight, Shane dragged a hand through his hair. If he was to win her over, persuasion had to be doled out in degrees of charm and skill.

Putting aside his frustration, Shane forced his heart-beat to slow to the same rhythmic cadence as the tick-tick-tick coming from the clock on the mantel behind him.

"Please, Miss Marley," he said, curving a pleasant

smile along the edges of his mouth. "I only ask that you hold off making a final decision until you hear me out."

Her gaze remained direct and unwavering. But instead of responding right away, she clamped her lips shut and scrunched her forehead into a web of hard, vertical lines.

Shane felt his chest heave. Trying to gauge how best to present his argument, he dropped a glance over the woman in one quick swoop. Dressed in a drab gray dress and equally uninspired shoes, her bland brown hair looked as if it might have corroded onto her head. Her starched collar matched her rigid spine. In fact, she sat so straight and so far back in her chair, Shane was amazed the pattern from the upholstery hadn't tattooed itself to her dress.

When he raised his gaze to meet hers, the cold eyes and pursed lips reminded him of the women he'd encountered throughout his childhood on the streets of New York City.

His instinct was to dismiss her at once. But he owed it to everyone involved to put his own feelings aside and conduct this interview with polite professionalism.

Taking another moment to control his emotions, Shane lowered his chin and scanned the references he held in his hand. He couldn't deny Miss Marley had the nursing experience he needed in an assistant. Her background was without blemish, her training impeccable. But did she have the temperament required for the unique position he offered?

There was one way to find out.

"The Charity House orphans are—"

"*Orphans?*" Her eyes went narrow and frosty, while her lips curled with pitch-perfect disgust. "You use that term loosely, Dr. Bartlett."

A muscle shifted in his jaw and Shane felt his smile slip.

Let the children come to me, and do not hinder them, for the Kingdom of God belongs to such as these...

At the reminder of Jesus's words, Shane had to fight back a wave of resentment at the woman's sanctimonious attitude.

"Perhaps they are not orphans in the literal sense," he acknowledged with a grim twist of his lips. "However, they are children who—"

She snorted. She actually *snorted* at him. The sound was harsh enough to stop him in midsentence.

"These children." He paused to emphasize his point, but then a dull drumming pounded in his ears and the pattern on the rug at his feet bled into a kaleidoscope of chaotic colors. Shane shook his head and began again. "These *children*...deserve decent medical care like everyone else."

She pierced him with a sharp look and spoke as though she hadn't heard his words. "This is a house for harlots' mistakes." She lifted her nose and looked pointedly around her. "Is it not, Dr. Bartlett?"

Before responding, Shane followed her gaze as it moved beyond the Persian rugs, past the expensive furniture, and straight to the crystal vases filled with fresh-cut flowers. The attention to detail was impossible to miss. Charity House was like no other orphanage in the territory, incomparable in its elegance and style.

And yet, Shane wondered if he'd made a mistake in choosing the mansion's front parlor as the place to conduct his interviews today.

He'd hoped that by showing the candidates the interior of the orphanage they would realize Charity House and its occupants had class and substance. Apparently, instead of unleashing this nursing candidate's compassion, he'd opened her judgment.

Whispered reminders of his own childhood crept forward in his mind. Shane clenched his jaw, refusing to allow this woman to see his growing anger until he had the poisonous emotion under control.

He forced his shoulders to relax.

"Whatever you might think of these children, remember they did not choose their parents," he said, surprised to hear his calm tone when so many ugly emotions churned just under the surface. "As I said before, they deserve equal and fair medical treatment."

He pierced her with a hard look, daring her to argue.

She blinked. Blinked again. Swallowed. Then slowly nodded. "I will concede your point, doctor. However, the children's situation notwithstanding, I am entitled to know about your other patients. What of the mothers still alive, the ones working in the brothels on Market Street?"

Shane held her stare. "I treat them, as well. And anyone else in need. I turn none away."

A sound of outrage slipped from her lips. "Innocent children are one thing, but their mothers are quite another. You did not say in your advertisement that you care for…for…sinners."

Her words were like a solid punch to his gut. How often had he heard similar accusations thrown at his own mother, all because she had chosen to be a wealthy man's mistress?

Memories lurking below the surface bubbled forth, taunting him. Shane's breath turned cold in his lungs under the assault.

Yes, his mother had been a sinner, but she had paid dearly for her mistakes. She'd died in shame, and there had been nothing Shane could do to stop the tragedy.

He'd been too young, too inexperienced, too—

Another unladylike sniff yanked him back to the present.

"You have nothing else to say to me, doctor?" she asked. "What is your defense for misleading me into thinking this was an ordinary nursing position?" The chill of her tone sat heavy in the room between them.

Shane fought to keep his resentment and anger from taking control of his reason. What had he been thinking, to allow this interview to continue so long?

He could never subject the Charity House children, their mothers, or any of his patients for that matter, to this woman and her…judgment.

He owed it to the memory of his own mother to find a compassionate nurse to assist him in his practice. Was guilt driving him to care for the disenfranchised? Guilt over failing the one woman who had sacrificed her life for him. Or was it true conviction that pushed him to care for the unwanted?

He wasn't sure anymore. Nor was he convinced his

motives mattered. His patients, and their care, had to come first.

With his mind made up, Shane rose from his chair and waited until the woman did the same. "Thank you for your time, Miss Marley. I am no longer in need of your services."

He did not offer her his hand.

"You are dismissing *me?*" The woman had the nerve to look mutinous, as though she was being unfairly sent away. "But you need my assistance. You said so yourself at the beginning of this interview."

With each breath he took, his patience wore thinner. "I think it is best we part ways at this juncture."

Gasping, she threw her shoulders back and lifted her chin high in the air. "I'm your last candidate," she said. "You have no one else."

"I am confident God will provide."

"You will regret this," she warned.

Shane met her gaze with an unrelenting glare of his own. "I will not."

He'd never spoken truer words. For although he knew things would get worse before they got better, he also knew he just needed a little more faith, a little more patience. All would work for the best.

With a loud huff, Miss Eugenia Marley skimmed her ice-edged gaze across him, turned on her heel and marched out of the room. Each angry step she took sounded like a hammer hitting unforgiving iron.

Shane stood stock-still, staring straight ahead. He

barely flinched when she slammed the door behind her with a loud bang.

For several moments he remained unmoving, looking out the window facing the backyard of Charity House. The wind beat at the glass with an angry fist, sending an unrelenting howl past a crack between the pane and wood casing.

A perfect expression of his own frustration.

There was no one left to interview. Shane could only hope that—

No. He would not waste precious energy on hope. Nor would he worry.

He would trust.

Rolling his shoulders, Shane shoved a hand through his hair and shut his eyes. He let the tension drain from him for a single moment. And then another. And another still. Waiting until his mind cleared enough to focus on prayer.

At last, he whispered, "Lord, I cannot do this alone. Where man fails, I know You excel. I pray You bless my patients with a compassionate woman to assist us."

Opening his eyes, Shane looked around the parlor room of Charity House. At first glance nobody would think this large and fancy mansion housed over forty children with nowhere else to go. Marc and Laney Dupree had created a home filled with compassion and caring, a refuge for the abandoned and unwanted boys and girls no other orphanage would touch.

The Duprees' generosity of spirit humbled Shane and inspired him to expand his own medical practice in the same vein, a practice that was becoming unmanageable for one man.

Trust. He had to trust that God had a plan. The Lord would bring relief in His perfect time.

A deep clearing of a throat jerked Shane out of his reverie. Pivoting at the sound, he locked his gaze with Marc Dupree's concerned expression. Dressed in a brocade vest and matching tie, with his dark hair immaculately combed and face clean shaven, Marc looked more like a banker than the fierce proprietor of an orphanage. But just like Charity House, Shane knew the other man had hidden depths, and was an example of complete integrity.

"Any success?" Marc asked.

Shane shook his head at his friend, and jammed his hands in his pockets. "It appears I've wasted another day with fruitless interviews." He lifted a shoulder in a helpless gesture. "Perhaps—"

A high-pitched scream cut off his words, followed by a round of incomprehensible shouting. Shane's ears pricked when he heard one voice rise above the others. "Somebody find Dr. Shane. Hurry."

Bella pivoted in several directions, searching desperately for the source of the panicked cries tumbling over one another.

Forcing herself to remain calm, she took a deep breath, stood immobile and listened intently. The shouts were coming from behind her.

She spun around and gasped at the sight before her.

Chaos had erupted in the massive yard that backed up to her brother's church.

Heart in her throat, Bella lurched forward. Stopped. Frowned.

Hadn't she learned from her recent experience with William that it was better to assess a situation before rushing headlong into the unknown?

Dreadful memories of her last meeting with the viscount slammed through her mind, washing away her concentration. She shook her head violently and gritted her teeth so hard her jaw hurt. Bella knew she should find the source of the disaster unraveling in front of her. Instead, exhaustion, shame and anger at William's betrayal threatened to steal her focus.

No. No, no, no. William would not invade her thoughts today.

Breathe, Bella, breathe.

One heartbeat passed.

And another.

By the third, Bella had taken in the stylish mansion at the opposite end of the yard. The fairy-tale backdrop was at odds with the trouble riding along the stiff mountain breeze. She counted over fifteen children of various sizes colliding into one another. Like waves crashing onto a beach, they plunged toward a common point—a child lying flat on his back.

Bella curled her fingers into fists. Where was the adult in charge?

Tossing her reticule to the ground, she sprinted toward the clump of frightened children. She'd barely taken two steps when a young girl of about ten years of age skidded to a stop at her side. The child had halted so abruptly that her shiny black pigtails swung forward and then landed with a soft thump on her narrow shoulders. Eyes wild and unfocused, her little cupid mouth worked quickly, but no sound came out.

Bella stooped to the girl's height and touched her shoulder. "Deep breaths, sweetie. Take one at a time."

Nodding, the girl gulped in large chunks of air.

"That's it," Bella said. "Now tell me what's happened."

"It's…it's…" She broke off and looked frantically around her.

Bella rolled her shoulders and prayed for patience. "It's…" she prompted in what she hoped was a soothing tone.

"My. Brother. *Ethan.*" She pointed to the cluster of children knotted around a small boy lying on the ground. "He hurt his leg. You gotta get Dr. Shane for me."

"Where?"

The girl cocked her head toward the mansion behind her. "Inside."

Bella placed her palm on the child's cheek. "Don't worry. I'll get him." Rising, she gave the girl's shoulder an encouraging squeeze. "You see to your brother. And whatever you do, make sure he doesn't move until the doctor gets there."

As though she hadn't heard a word Bella said, the child stabbed her gaze back to her brother, over to the large house behind her, then back to her brother again.

"Did you hear me?" Bella asked.

The girl nodded. Gulped. Gulped again. Then finally—*finally*—she lifted her chin and lurched toward the injured boy.

Bella whirled in the direction of the house. At the same moment, two large men exited the backdoor in a run.

Bella faltered in her steps, froze. In her stunned state, she only had time for impressions. Both men were tall. Dark-haired. Broad-shouldered. One was dressed in expensive clothing that would make her flamboyant brother Tyler fall to his knees and weep with envy. The other wore a nondescript white shirt and black pants and carried a small black bag.

Dr. Shane.

The calm in his manner gave Bella such a sense of relief she pressed a hand to her throat and sighed. This man would make everything better.

The young girl changed directions and dashed to the bottom of the porch steps. "Ethan's hurt, Dr. Shane." She grasped his hand and tugged. "You gotta come quick."

The sharp planes of his face tensed and his mouth pressed into a tight line. Yet, he carefully patted the girl on her back. "Don't worry, Molly. I'll take care of him." His smooth baritone was pitched to the perfect level to instill calm. "You concentrate on finding your mother and father and then bring them here."

"Right." Teetering from one foot to the other, arms flailing, the child found her center at last and set off at a terrifying pace.

Focused on his task once more, the doctor lengthened his strides. With each step, his gaze shifted over the scene, taking note of every detail. He measured, assessed. Picked up the pace.

The other man followed hard on his heels.

Negotiating the final few feet, the doctor gently set two of the smaller children to one side and then dropped to his knees. "Marc," he threw over his shoulder. "I need room."

The fancy-dressed man went to work at once. With an authoritative tone and in-charge manner, he organized the children into two work groups. In perfect rhythm they shifted away from the injured boy, picked up toys, balls, shoes and began setting them into neat piles.

They were so purposeful in their task, so obedient, even as the nightmare churned around them, that Bella found herself gaping.

What sort of children were these? And then she remembered her brother's many letters telling her about the unique orphanage that shared the church's backyard. Charity Home. No. Charity House. Yes, that was the name.

Before she could take another look at the mansion-turned-orphanage, the doctor darted his gaze along the perimeter of the yard as though he was searching for something. Or someone. A helper, perhaps? Before Bella could offer her assistance, his eyes locked on to hers.

Snared in his powerful stare, her lungs constricted. Although she was too far away to make out the individual features of his face, the impact of all that intensity thrown her way had her stepping sharply back.

"You, there," he said, his features twisting into a frown of concentration. "I need your assistance."

Jolted into action, Bella yanked off one glove and

then another. "Yes, of course." By the time she'd crossed the yard, she'd tossed her hat to the ground, as well.

The children continued to chatter softly as they made room for the doctor to work. Their voices rose slightly as they began trooping one by one inside the large house but it was all background noise now. Never taking her attention off the boy, Bella knelt beside him and looked into his small, pale face.

Glassy eyes stared back at her. She swallowed down a gasp of surprise. He was so young, no more than four or five, with black curly hair and big brown eyes.

Lord, please ease this child's pain. Use me as your instrument to erase his suffering.

Unsure what to do next, she waited for specific instructions from the doctor. When none came, a shiver of foreboding iced across her skin.

Cautiously, she lifted her gaze. And found herself staring into ocean-blue eyes the exact color as William's.

Unwelcome images swirled through her mind like leaves on a deserted street. Incapable of grasping any one thought before it was replaced by another, her mind drained into a black void of nothingness.

Air clogged in her lungs.

Focus, Bella. Focus, focus, focus.

The doctor must have sensed her internal struggle because his eyes narrowed to inscrutable slits.

Bella quickly lowered her gaze back to the hurt boy. Little Ethan's eyes were ringed with pain. Tears wavered on the edges of his lashes, but he gritted his teeth and released a shaky sigh.

"Oh, you brave little boy." Bella touched his cheek softly then brushed the sweaty hair off his forehead with her fingertips. "You're going to be fine. Just fine."

As though her words gave him permission to give into the pain, the tears spilled from his eyes. "It…it hurts," he gasped, his young voice shaking with anguish. "Real bad."

Bella stroked her hand along his hairline. "I know it does, baby. But the doctor is going to make it better."

Shutting out all thoughts but this small, helpless child, she boldly returned her gaze to the doctor's face. "Isn't that right, Dr. Shane?"

The sun chose that moment to break through a slit in the fast-moving clouds. Big. Hot. Illuminating.

The doctor stared at her for a long, tense moment. This time, Bella couldn't look away. The bold, aristocratic angles of his cheekbones, the finely shaped nose and strong jaw covered with day-old stubble created a handsome portrait any leading man would covet.

Bella blinked.

Slowly—very, *very* slowly—Dr. Shane dropped his gaze to the child. "I'll do my best, Ethan."

The boy let out another shaky sigh. "I know."

Dr. Shane cut his gaze back to Bella. "Let's get to work, shall we?"

His words were more statement than question, but there was an edge of doubt in his eyes. He was asking her to assist him, daring her perhaps, yet convinced she'd somehow let him down.

Would she? She had no training, no experience. Yet an injured boy needed her.

Lord, give me the courage to do what is needed.

Fortunately, the very moment she ended her prayer, Bella's worries fell away. All that remained was a driving sense of purpose.

She swallowed back the last shreds of uncertainty and boldly held Dr. Shane's gaze. "Tell me what to do."

Chapter Two

Locked inside that startling amber gaze, Shane's thoughts morphed into one undeniable realization. She hadn't hesitated. The woman with the dark, golden curls, flawless features and refined British accent had defied his expectations. Instead of fleeing the unpleasantness of a child's injury, she'd taken her place without question.

Could she be the answer to his prayer?

Wishful thinking at best. It was far too soon to determine if she had the character and necessary qualifications he required in an assistant.

Yet, even now, as she boldly held his gaze, conviction blazed in her eyes. *What eyes. What depth of emotion.*

His heart kicked hard against his ribs, warning him to beware of this woman, this *stranger.*

Lifting a perfectly arched eyebrow at him, she blew out a slow, impatient breath. "I'm ready whenever you are."

It took another few seconds for Shane to empty the overload of thoughts and impressions twining together in his mind. "Tell me where it hurts, Ethan."

The little boy moaned in response, pain twisting his young face. "My...my leg."

"Let's have a look."

Careful to keep his features bland, Shane flicked his gaze past the boy's torso. Shane's first reflex was to pull in a sharp breath. Instead, he detached. Separated emotion from logic. And focused.

The right pant leg had been torn at a jagged, vertical angle. Blood soaked the material, turning the light brown cloth nearly black.

"Don't move, Ethan." He flipped open his medical bag. "I have to cut away the material surrounding the wound."

"Oh...okay."

Shane's chest pinched tight at the sound of the boy's anguish. *Oh, Lord,* he prayed. *Fill me with Your Spirit. Guide my hands and use me as Your instrument for healing.*

With slow, careful movements, Shane set a firm grip on Ethan's thigh, and then looked up at the woman again. "I need you to keep him calm for me."

Eyes wide, she sank her teeth into her lower lip. "How?"

"Hold his hand. Speak to him." Shane lifted a shoulder. "Whatever it takes."

Nodding, she braided her fingers with the boy's. "Ethan. I want you to concentrate on me." She waited for him to turn his head toward her. "That's it. The doctor is going to have a look at your injury. Nothing more."

Ethan sucked in big gulps of air. "I'm scared."

"I know," she said, her voice barely above a whisper. "Me, too."

Shane wanted to tell them both that everything would be fine, but he couldn't make such a promise. Not yet.

"You talk funny," Ethan announced. "I like it."

Shane did, too. The proper British accent suited her.

"Why, thank you, Ethan. I like the way you talk, too." Leaning toward the boy's ear, she asked, "Do you have a favorite song?"

His dark brows pulled together in a frown of concentration. "I...lots... I don't know...maybe... 'Amazing Grace'?"

She smiled her approval. "I like that one, too."

In a low, hushed tone, she began the hymn. Her soft, lilting voice was no piercing soprano as Shane half expected. Rather, she sang with a rich, smoky timbre. Pure velvety warmth. The perfect alto to calm the beast in any man. Or boy.

As Ethan's leg relaxed under Shane's touch, Shane found the restlessness inside him also stopping, pausing. Listening to the beautiful song.

Torn between shock and admiration, Shane shook his head and returned to his work. With quick snips, he cut away the tattered material and pulled it aside to reveal a long, nasty gash running down the side of Ethan's leg. Thankfully, there was no swelling or misshapen bump to indicate a break.

As if on cue, the woman turned her gaze toward the injury, as well. To her credit, her singing never faltered. Nor did she flinch.

Astounding.

Shane had seen trained doctors fail to maintain their reactions so well. Stunned once again by her remarkable behavior, Shane sucked in a lungful of cold mountain air. Who was this woman? He was certain he'd never met her. Then why did he experience recognition when he looked into her eyes?

The sound of approaching footsteps cut off his thoughts.

Stabbing a glance over his shoulder, Shane barked out a set of orders for Marc. "I'm going to move Ethan to the kitchen. I'll need water, clean rags and Laney's sewing kit."

Having experienced his share of injuries, Marc pivoted on his heel and flicked his wrist in the air. "I'm already on it."

"Ethan, before we move you I want to make sure you haven't broken anything."

The boy squeezed his eyes shut, sighed. "I'm ready."

"This might hurt," Shane warned.

At his words, the woman stopped singing. Shane silently willed her to resume her impromptu musical. Instead, she gently stroked the child's hair along his forehead. "I don't think I've ever met a braver boy than you, and I've been all over the world."

Ethan cracked open one eye and then the other. "You have? Wh…where?"

Her expression never changed nor did her rhythmic stroking of his hair. "Lots of places."

"Tell me. Tell me," he demanded with little-boy earnestness.

"Let's see." She tapped her chin with a fingertip. "Paris. London. Ro—"

"London?" Ethan tried to sit up, but she gently pushed him back down.

"I've always wanted to go to London," he declared. "To see the Tower and all."

Both grinning, they began a lengthy discussion of the infamous prison.

While Ethan babbled, Shane took the opportunity to check for broken bones. "Tell me if it hurts when I press on your leg."

"What's your name?" Ethan asked once he wound down his list of reasons for seeing the Tower of London.

Eager to hear her response himself, Shane turned an ear in their direction and ran his hand across Ethan's leg.

"I'm Bella," she declared.

Italian for beautiful. The name suited her. Shane moved his fingers along the boy's kneecap.

"Bella," Ethan said, his face scrunched in confusion. "I've never heard that name before."

She released a tinkling laugh, the sound as clear and musical as her singing. "It's short for Isabella."

Holding back a grin at the look of adoration in the young boy's eyes, Shane moved to the calf.

"Actually," she said. "My full name is Isabella Constance O'Toole, but you can call me Bella."

Ethan jerked.

Shane froze. "Did I hurt you?"

Ethan ignored the question. "*O'Toole?* That's Pastor Beau's last name."

Laughing again, she gave the boy a dazzling smile. "I know. He's my brother."

Shane took a quick pull of air into his lungs. Of course she was the reverend's sister. The similarity was hard to miss, now that he looked. They had the same golden hair, same tawny eyes, same memorable, aristocratic features. Perhaps that explained the odd sense of recognition every time their eyes met.

Shane finished his exam by searching for any obstruction or object lodged in the wound. Satisfied at last, he hopped to his feet and lifted the boy in his arms. "Let's get you inside."

"Don't leave me, Miss Bella." Struggling, Ethan reached out his hands to her.

"Not to worry, Ethan." She rose and closed her fingers over his. "I'm not going anywhere. You're my priority right now."

A burning throb knotted in Shane's stomach. There was a time in his life when he would have given anything to hear those same words uttered directly at him.

Closing his mind to the unwelcome thought, Shane repositioned the boy in his arms. Without being told, Miss O'Toole grabbed his medical bag and stuffed the scissors inside.

The three of them entered the kitchen, Miss O'Toole leading the way. Shane shouldered the door shut behind them and then took a cursory look around.

The room was empty. Unusual for this time of day. But before Shane could speculate further, Marc entered with an armful of clean linens and set them on the center counter.

"Where's your wife?" Shane asked.

Marc shot him an apologetic glance. "Laney and Mrs. Smythe went shopping for supplies. And Megan is upstairs organizing the children for naptime." He began rolling up his sleeves. "That leaves me as your only helper at the moment."

"And Miss Bella, too," Ethan added.

"And Miss Bella, too," Shane said without looking at the woman. He found looking at her distracted him.

Setting Ethan on the counter, he picked up a cloth off the pile Marc had set down.

Using the clean water out of the bucket, Shane washed the blood from Ethan's wound, revealing good news and bad. The good news—the cut was indeed free of any debris. But the bad news was as disheartening as Shane had feared. The large gash would need stitching to close the wound.

A crash from upstairs had all three adults jumping. Marc shook his head in resignation. "I better check on that." He turned to Miss O'Toole, who was standing slightly back but within eyeshot of Ethan. "Looks like you'll have to assist Shane without me."

She stepped forward, her gaze filled with fierce determination. "Of course. I'll do whatever is needed."

Marc smiled at her, a look of relief filling his features. "Thank you." He leaned over Ethan, touched the boy's arm. "Hang tough, little man. No doubt your parents will be here soon. In the meantime, Dr. Shane and Miss Bella are going to fix you up."

Ethan's lower lip quivered. "Okay."

After sharing a quick look with Shane, Marc left the room.

Miss O'Toole smiled after him. "Nice man," she muttered.

Shane swallowed back a surprising kick of jealousy and rummaged through Laney's sewing kit for a needle and thread. "Can you sew, Miss O'Toole?"

His voice must have come out harder than he'd planned because she took a sharp step back, and eyed him with a healthy dose of wariness. "I've been sewing my own costumes since I was twelve."

"Good. I'll need you to stitch the wound for me." He spoke over her shocked gasp. "You'll make individual stitches, knotting and cutting them off one at a time before beginning the next."

She slid a quick glance at the angry wound. Shivered. "Can't you do it?"

If only he could. But he knew the procedure would be painful, painful enough that Ethan would need holding down. "I'll have to…keep him still."

Her eyes widened in instant understanding. *"Oh."*

Shane closed his fingers over hers. The unexpected warmth that spread from her palm to his had him quickly releasing her. "I'll talk you through it," he promised.

She nodded, flexed the hand he'd just held. Nodded again. "All right, then."

Ethan whimpered at her declaration. "Will it hurt, Miss Bella?"

Sighing, she trailed the back of her fingertips down his cheek. "A little, but I'll work as quickly as possible."

"Fine." Ethan squeezed his eyes shut once again and took a deep, shaky breath. "Do what you must." The adult words were completely at odds with the childish hiccupping that followed.

Shane passed the needle and thread to Miss O'Toole. With slow, deliberate movements, he placed one hand on Ethan's shoulder and the other on the thigh of the boy's injured leg. For now, he kept his touch light, and would only increase the pressure when needed.

After threading the needle, she leaned forward and placed a kiss on the boy's head. The lingering scent of jasmine and sandalwood brought a vague memory dancing on the edges of Shane's mind.

He shut it down.

Miss O'Toole met his gaze with honest trepidation in her eyes. No coyness. No pretend confidence.

Shane gave her a heartening smile. "Let's begin."

Bella's hands might be shaking, her heart might be pounding faster than a series of half notes, but she was getting the job done as quickly as she could.

"Only one more to go," the doctor encouraged. "You're doing fine."

She appreciated his support, more than he probably knew. This task went far beyond her capabilities. But prayer and this man's precise instructions had gotten her through the worst.

Gritting her teeth, she tied off the final knot. "There." She released her breath and placed her hand on Ethan's shoulder. "All done."

"That…" The little boy's bottom lip quivered. "Wasn't so bad." The tear tracks down his face told a different story.

The realization that she'd hurt a child, in spite of the necessity, weighed heavy in her throat, making her breath come in ragged pants.

Seeking reinforcement, or at least a nod of approval, she glanced at the doctor. But he wasn't paying attention to her. Head lowered, he blotted the remaining blood off Ethan's skin and then wrapped a series of plasters and strips of linen over the wound. It wasn't until he finished the task that he looked at her directly.

She sucked in a quick breath of air. The eyes that stared back at her were a deep, troubled blue.

What sort of inner strength did it take to administer necessary healing, even when it caused such pain? Certainly, it had to be a difficult life. Lonely, even. She felt a sudden urge to offer some show of compassion, give a kind word at least. But the doctor turned away and began cleaning up the mess they'd made.

Needing to do something, *anything* but stare at the man's rigid back, she whisked Ethan into her arms. Holding him tightly against her, she paced to the back corner of the kitchen and began humming the aria from *Tristan and Isolde.*

Ethan sniffled, then wiped his nose on her shoulder. "That really hurt, Miss Bella."

"I know, darling," she said. "But you were very, very brave."

He clung harder to her neck. "I don't ever want you to do that again."

A shudder ran through her and she tightened her hold. "Me neither. I'd rather—"

The door flew open with a bang. Bella spun toward the noise.

Two adults, one male, one female, spilled into the kitchen. The young girl from the yard trailed closely behind. Hidden in the shadows, Bella cast the three a quick, assessing look.

The man was tall, broad-shouldered and ominous-looking with his dark hair, dark eyes and dark-stubbled jaw. A tin star was pinned to his chest, making him look every bit the terrifying Wild West lawman of legend. The woman was smaller, softer, her coal-black hair and blue eyes a grown-up version of the girl clutching her hand.

Clearly, this was Ethan's family. All three—mother, father, sister—wore identical expressions of concern.

Patting Ethan's back, Bella moved out of the shadows.

The woman's eyes landed on the boy first. "Oh, baby," she cried. "My poor baby."

Ethan twisted toward the voice. "Mama."

He nearly launched himself out of Bella's arms. The momentum from his struggles flung them both forward.

Bella half handed, half dropped the squirming child into his mother's ready embrace.

The lawman moved just as quickly as Ethan had. Jaw tight, gaze locked with his wife's, he patted the boy on the back and whispered his own words of affection. For a tense moment, all thoughts and attention were on the sniffling little boy. Even his sister added her own soft words, patting the boy's back like her father did.

Once Ethan's sobs died down to sniffing hiccups, the father lowered his hand and leveled a hard glare on the doctor.

"What happened?"

His tone came out harsh, unrelenting, a father demanding a full accounting of his son's accident. Clearly, this man protected his own.

In clipped, short sentences, the doctor sketched out the details of the boy's injury. He ended with an explanation of Bella's role in caring for the child. "Miss O'Toole was good enough to step forward and sew the wound shut."

A pall of silence filled the room as all eyes turned toward her.

Unsure what to say, Bella simply stared back.

The little girl found her voice first. "Daddy, Daddy. She's the one I told you about, the one in the church's backyard."

He raised a questioning brow at Bella.

A dozen responses ran through her mind, but none seemed quite right. Bella curled her fingertips into her skirt and swallowed. Facing this stern, upset father was far harder than walking on stage in front of a hostile theater audience.

She had no experience to draw from.

As though sensing her unease, Dr. Shane caught her eye and gave her a quick, approving smile. Her stomach performed a perfect roll, and she found the confidence to speak. "I was very proud of your son," she said, careful to keep her voice from quivering. "He didn't kick out once."

Both parents smiled at her then. And to her surprise, she saw no judgment in their eyes. No condemnation. Just genuine appreciation. "Thank you, Miss—" The woman shook her head. "I'm sorry, but I didn't catch your name."

"It's Bella. Bella O'Toole." At the instant recognition in their eyes, Bella opened her mouth to explain but Ethan beat her to it.

"She's Pastor Beau's sister," he said with a look of pride in his eyes, as though he didn't often know something the others didn't.

At the news, the woman flashed a dazzling smile at Bella, a smile brilliant enough to reach the back row in any theater. "That's lovely. We think very highly of your brother."

"Yes, we do," the husband agreed.

The look of admiration in all their eyes told its own story. Who would have thought her brother, the only member of her family who had denied his place on the stage, would become so popular, so well-loved without ever singing a note or reciting a fictional phrase.

Because he was Beau. A man of solid, Christian integrity who ministered to the lost and hurting—the shamed.

People like Bella herself.

A wave of melancholy crashed through her. She suddenly wanted—*no, needed*—to see her big brother. Now.

But she couldn't leave yet. Could she?

Ethan's father stepped forward, ending her quandary. "I'm Trey Scott." He pointed to the woman standing closely behind him. "This is my wife, Katherine. You already know Ethan." He swiveled halfway around and pulled the girl closer. "And this is our daughter, Molly."

Tugging the child with him, he moved back to his wife's side.

Bella's heart ached at the picture the four made. Standing there like that, staring at her with such gratitude in their eyes, such peace and contentment in spite of Ethan's injury, they made a beautiful family.

Sadness, sorrow and a bone-deep sense of loss overwhelmed her all at once. She had dreamed of starting her own family—with William. But the viscount was living that dream with another woman.

Bella's heart broke a little more at the thought.

As though sensing her shift in mood, the little girl rushed forward and gripped Bella's hand. "Are you all right?" she asked. "You look like you're about to cry."

Bella angled her head to stare into the guileless face. "I...I'm fine."

But she lied. She wasn't fine. She hadn't been fine since she'd escaped London and William's ugly proposal.

Clicking her tongue, Katherine handed Ethan to her husband. The next thing Bella knew she was being pulled into the other woman's embrace. "Thank you," she whispered. "Thank you for taking care of my son."

Bella tried not to cling, but for one black moment she thought she might break down and cry. If she gave in to the urge, she might never stop.

At last, Katherine pushed back.

"I hope you will be staying in Denver awhile," she said.

No, Bella thought, as she took a farther step away from all that suffocating kindness. She didn't want to stay here with these nice people. She didn't deserve to stay. She wanted to run. And never look back. But where would she go? There were already too many secrets, and too many regrets that had followed her from London. Surely, they would follow her wherever she went.

"I'm here for an extended stay," she said once she had command over her voice again. Which, all things considered, was as truthful as she could be at the moment.

Katherine eyed her for a long moment, then nodded. "Good. I think you need to be here."

She spoke with such certainty, such compassion, Bella's hand flew to her throat. Her fingertips caught against the pendant William had given her, reminding her of her shame.

Why hadn't she thrown away the necklace?

As soon as the question arose, the answer came. Because the heavy pendant was a reminder of how close she'd come to committing adultery and how far she'd walked from her faith. Until her sins were washed clean, *if* they were washed clean, she would continue to wear the incriminating necklace.

As though mocking her, the wind scratched at the window with clawlike strokes. Bella wanted to rush into the raw air, wanted to feel the hard slap of sobering cold against her skin.

Her breaths started coming shorter, faster, harder.

To her horror, and in front of these kind people, Bella stood on the brink of panic.

Dr. Shane cleared his throat, saving her from making a fool of herself. With extraordinary patience, he waited until he had everyone's attention—including hers— before he began a litany of instructions needed to keep the boy's wound clean and infection free.

Bella tried to listen. Truly, she tried. But all the pain of the last month, all the nerves of the last few moments tangled into a tight knot in the pit of her stomach.

At last, the doctor finished his list of instructions and then turned his attention to her. "Miss O'Toole."

Bella bristled at the abrupt tone, ready to do battle, until she noted the hint of vulnerability in his gaze.

"Yes?"

He ran his hand through his hair. A gesture he clearly repeated often, if the messy edges were any indication. Instead of making him look foolish, the mussed hair added a hint of boyish charm to his otherwise too-handsome features.

"Miss O'Toole," he repeated. "Am I to understand you are in Denver for an indefinite period of time?"

He sounded so formal. So distant and cold. But there

was a hint of desperation in his tone, as well, and thus she found the courage to answer his question with complete honesty. "You are correct in your assumption."

The sincerity in his gaze gave her renewed hope.

But then he spoke. And condemned her all over again. "I have a proposition for you. One I pray you will consider with the utmost care."

Chapter Three

At last.

Shane had found a capable woman to assist him in his practice. But instead of feeling a sense of relief, a burst of unease pounded through his veins.

Miss O'Toole's face had gone dead white. She remained frozen in place, staring at him with ill-cocealed horror.

Had she misunderstood his intentions?

Shane rubbed a finger over his temple and fought down a second wave of uncertainty.

Grabbing a quick breath of air, he began again. "What I meant to say is…thank you. You did a fine job with Ethan today."

Her hand rose to her throat. She fiddled with the golden pendant around her neck while her gaze flitted around the kitchen, landing on nothing in particular.

Was she listening to him?

"We're all very grateful," Trey added with one of his rare smiles directed solely at her.

Unfortunately, the magnanimous gesture was lost on Miss O'Toole. She blinked rapidly now, sending the first glitter of tears wiggling along her long, spiky lashes.

Confused and terrified. Those were the words that came to mind as Shane tried to unravel her odd reaction to his request.

In truth, he sympathized.

He was battling his own sense of bewilderment, as though he, too, was on the cusp of diving into something beautiful and *terrible*.

"I haven't seen that steady of a hand in a long time," he continued. "You have a gift, Miss O'Toole."

Her shoulders stiffened at his compliment and some unknown emotion flashed in her eyes. Discomfort? Pleasure? Something else entirely? "I…I do?"

"Yes."

"I…" She lifted her chin, pulled in a composing breath. "Thank you."

Her uncertain manner was replaced by a quiet dignity.

Something inside Shane threatened to snap.

How could he want to protect the woman one moment and wish to rest in her strength the next?

Rest in her strength?

For a moment, the foundation of everything Shane thought rocked under him. He was a healer, called by God to treat the sick, a man others turned to in time of need. He did not rely on anyone.

No human, at any rate. Only the divine.

Then again, he'd never met a woman who made him want to release some of his tight control, to admit he might be weary of standing helplessly by as his patients struggled with illnesses that far too often resulted in death.

For the first time in his life, a woman—*a fancy, over-dressed, far too beautiful stranger*—made Shane want to share a little of his burdens with another person.

What did that say about him? About his faith in God as his only guide and one true hope?

"Miss O'Toole, I have an offer I would like to present you, a *job* offer," he hastened to add when she sucked in her breath a second time at his words. "What I ask is highly respectable."

Glancing from Trey's amused expression to Katherine's pitiful shaking of her head, Shane shifted his stance and continued. "Would you consider working as my assistant?"

Instead of answering him, she looked at Katherine who tossed her palms in the air and shrugged. The gesture seemed to say: who can understand what men really want from us women?

They shared a smile of feminine understanding. Or maybe it was a grimace. Either way, a thousand words passed between them, words no mere man could hope to understand.

There was another long pause, during which Miss O'Toole released a sigh and turned back.

"You want me to be your assistant, nothing else?" Her eyes narrowed with suspicion.

Shane shoved a hand through his hair. "Nothing else, I assure you."

She blinked at him, opened her mouth, closed it again. And so the staring began again.

What was wrong with the woman?

Clearing his throat, Trey resettled Ethan in his arms and glanced at his wife. "I think we should leave these two to their discussion."

The marshal's suggestion was innocent enough, but the casual alertness of his posture said he'd been listening to every word spoken, and a few unspoken, as well.

Nodding, Katherine murmured something Shane didn't quite catch before she turned to Molly. "Come on, Moll." She plucked one of her daughter's pigtails. "Let's get Ethan home and in bed."

"But it's still daylight," the little boy whined as he struggled in his father's arms. "I want to stay and play with the kids."

Kicking with remarkable strength, his face was a contorted mixture of childish rebellion and youthful disappointment.

"You've had a bad time of it, baby." Katherine reached out in silent command to her husband. Trey handed the boy over with the patience of a man used to obliging his wife's wishes.

As they made the exchange, Shane marveled at the silent harmony between Trey and Katherine Scott. The couple had created a happy, tight-knit family out of impossible odds. If Shane ever doubted God's ability to heal the wounded and bring about good from tragedy, all he had to do was look at this unified family for proof.

"Please, let me stay." Ethan's voice squeaked along the edge of a loud sob.

"You need to rest for a while, little man," Trey said in a placating tone with a firm hand on the boy's back. "Then we'll see how you feel."

He shot his wife a challenging look over Ethan's head. "Isn't that right, darling?"

"We'll discuss it, *after* his nap," she said, her voice no less formidable for its soft tone.

A stalemate began.

But as was often the case, the ruthless lawman who could intimidate murdering outlaws without flinching capitulated under his wife's unyielding stare. "Whatever you say, dear."

Katherine gave her husband a pleased smile. "I knew you'd see things my way."

"What can I say?" Trey returned the look with another long, intent stare. "I'm an accommodating man."

She giggled. She actually giggled. This, from the same woman who ruled her schoolroom with iron-clad structure.

Shane tried not to gape.

Molly rolled her gaze to the ceiling and groaned.

Silently agreeing with the girl, Shane handed Trey a roll of linen bandages. "Use these to wrap the leg once you've cleaned his wound in the morning. I'll be by to check on him in the afternoon."

"Right."

Before the Scott family filed out, Miss O'Toole summoned a brisk air of confidence and said, "Let me know if there's anything I can do, as well."

"We will," Trey answered for them all. "And thank you again, Miss O'Toole. For everything." One side of his mouth kicked up and he gave her a gallant bow, one more suited for a ballroom back east than a well-worn kitchen.

"It was my pleasure." She dropped her gaze to Molly, touched the girl's shoulder. "You were very brave today."

The little girl flushed. "He's my brother."

Miss O'Toole squeezed the child's shoulder in understanding then dropped her hand. Sighing, she walked over to Ethan and rubbed his back. There was such tenderness in her hands, such sweetness in her smile Shane found himself as riveted as Ethan appeared to be.

"Will you come see me, too, Miss Bella?" the boy asked. "With Dr. Shane?"

"I'll do my best."

Katherine patted Ethan's bottom. "All right, folks, enough stalling. Let's go." She touched Bella's arm and smiled. "Thank you again."

One by one the Scott family trooped out the backdoor with Ethan waving enthusiastically over his mother's head.

Once the door banged shut, Shane was far too aware of the silence as Miss O'Toole turned back to face him.

Their gazes locked with a force that nearly flattened him. In that moment, he forgot about steady hands and compassionate hearts and all the other reasons he'd decided Miss O'Toole would do nicely in the role of assistant.

He had one clear goal now: to convince this woman to work with him, by his side, for as long as possible.

What if she says no?

Desperation at the thought came so strong, so quick, Shane staggered back a step.

Cocking her head, Miss O'Toole pulled her eyebrows into a delicate frown. "I'm afraid I don't quite understand what you're asking of me."

Shane started forward, hesitated, shoved a hand through his hair. "It's quite simple. My practice is growing faster than I can keep up. I'm in need of someone to assist me in—"

"No, no." She waved her hand in a vague gesture. "I understand that part. What I don't quite fathom is why me?"

A ripple of unease slipped down his throat. Blunt honesty was the only way now. Shane stuffed his hands in his pockets and rocked back on his heels. "I started this practice to provide medical care for the women and children no other doctor would touch. It's—"

"Yes, yes, my brother told me about Charity House and the unique children living here. I also know some aren't actually orphans." Her chin lifted. "I have a good idea of the sort of patients you see."

He ignored how the sunlight streaming in from the window shone off her hair, how it twinkled in her gingerbread eyes. But he could not ignore the relief he experienced at her words. She knew all about Charity House, every squalid detail. And yet, she wasn't running in the opposite direction.

This could only be an answer to prayer.

Thank You, Lord.

"Life is difficult for the defenseless ones in this world," he said. "Regardless of life choices, everyone deserves medical care."

"All the more reason to make sure you hire the right person."

"I believe I am."

She wrapped her arms around her waist. "I still don't understand why you want me?"

Her voice was steady, but there was something in her gaze that told him his answer was far more important than merely convincing her she was the right person for the temporary position.

She needed reassurance.

He wouldn't have thought that of her. But whatever secret she harbored—and yes, she held a dark secret in her heart—it had destroyed a portion of her confidence.

A small, still voice told him to go forth with faith. "Perhaps I don't know everything about you, but remember I witnessed you in action today. You never hesitated, you followed directions precisely. You're Pastor O'Toole's sister. And you—"

Before he could expand further, the backdoor swung open and in strode the very man he'd just mentioned.

Unfortunately, Reverend Beauregard O'Toole's face was twisted in alarm. "Where is she?" he demanded, drilling his gaze into Shane. "I heard my sister is here but I don't believe it."

With each word the preacher spoke Miss O'Toole

took a step back, nearly blending into the shadows of the outer edges of the kitchen. Her tawny eyes became like soiled glass, completely concealing her emotions.

With growing curiosity, Shane watched her odd retreat.

Following Shane's gaze with his own, Beau swung around and caught sight of his sister. "Bella?" He moved in her direction. "Bella! It is you."

"Beau." She took a tentative step forward, two back, another forward, then rushed across the kitchen floor and flung herself into his arms. "Oh, Beau. I've missed you."

Wrapping her tightly in his arms, he patted her back much like a parent would a child. "Ah, Bella," he said. "It's been too long."

She sniffed, buried her face against his shoulder.

After countless seconds, Beau pulled back and very slowly, *very* carefully set her away from him. He studied her face a moment longer, then frowned. "What's happened?"

She gripped the pendant around her neck and tapped her collarbone lightly with her fist. "Nothing's happened," she said, her voice nonchalant. *Too nonchalant.*

Beau folded his arms over his chest. "Try again, little sister."

She dropped her gaze to her toes and dug the tip of her boot into a slat in the wood floor. "Can't a girl visit her brother and meet his new wife without there being a reason?"

Shane sighed. Whatever had brought Bella O'Toole to Denver she wasn't going to share the details with her brother anytime soon. Pity, that. Shane knew from personal experience the unholy tragedies that grew out of hidden secrets.

"No, Bella." Beau gently clutched his sister by the shoulders. "A woman does not travel halfway around the world to see her brother without a reason. Not when she's on tour in Europe." He placed a finger under her chin and applied pressure. "Not when she's been given the role of a lifetime."

Chin up, she glanced desperately at Shane out of the corners of her eyes. He lifted a shoulder in a helpless gesture. In return, her face took on a look of feminine determination, the personification of "watch this."

Shane's stomach did a fast roll.

Unconsciously regal, she crossed the kitchen and stood next to Shane, shoulder to shoulder, in a show of solidarity. *Take that big brother,* her stance said. *It's us against you.*

Shane's stomach did another, faster roll.

Right. He was in the thick of it now, caught in the middle of a sibling squabble full of dynamics he didn't fully understand.

Miss O'Toole slid him a quicksilver grin, took a deep breath.

Shane braced for impact.

"As of today," she said on a breezy whisper, turning those remarkable eyes onto her brother. "I no longer sing opera."

The dramatic lilt of her voice made Shane visibly cringe. A scene was in the making.

Thankfully, as a member of a famous acting family,

Beauregard O'Toole had seen his share of female theatrics. And like any big brother worth his salt, he didn't seem overly impressed with his sister's performance.

"Just like that. No more opera." His tone flattened. "One day in Denver and you quit your life's calling."

With elegant movements, she reached out, took a deep breath and smoothed a loose strand of hair off her face. "Who said singing opera is my life's calling?" she asked.

Beau's eyes narrowed to thin slits. "You did. In every letter you've written since you turned twelve years old."

Ah, the rare valid point in the midst of female illogic. A point, Shane noted, that Miss O'Toole completely disregarded with an unladylike sniff. "As of today," she wrapped her arm through Shane's, "I'm a nurse."

Beau sucked in a breath. "You're a *what?*"

"A. Nurse," she said through clenched teeth.

"Assistant, actually," Shane muttered.

Both O'Tooles glared at him.

"There's a difference," Shane pointed out, his voice sounding defensive even to his own ears. "A rather large difference," he added with more confidence as he untangled his arm from Miss O'Toole's.

"You hired Bella?" Beau's gaze cut through Shane like a scalpel. "Have you gone mad?"

Shane glanced at the woman standing beside him, noted the hidden desperation behind her false bravado. For whatever reason, she needed this job—he knew it as sure as he knew his own name—and Shane Bartlett was a fool for a woman in need.

No matter what that meant to his friendship with

Beau, no matter how ill-thought out the idea was, Shane was going to hire Bella O'Toole as his new assistant.

"Apparently." He blew out a frustrated hiss. "Insanity is indeed one of my more stellar traits."

Chapter Four

Alone at last in her brother's house, belongings long since stowed in the guest bedroom, Bella stood in the small, beautifully decorated parlor. Ignoring the lace curtains, the rose-print wallpaper and stylish furniture, she placed her hand on the windowpane, leaned her forehead on the cool glass and simply looked at the scenery beyond.

The slow ticking from the clock on the mantel soothed her nerves. She found herself slowing her breathing to match the rhythmic cadence.

She hadn't expected to find Beau settled in the middle of a wealthy neighborhood. He'd written in great detail of his decision to build a church that would be directly connected to an orphanage for prostitutes' mistakes. He'd told of his wife's support, both financial and emotional, throughout the entire building project. But his letters had failed to do justice to the fairy-tale world in which they'd settled.

And not just the large homes of expensive brick, manicured lawns and attention to detail.

Bella had never seen a sky so blue. So clear.

The mountains in the distance marched in a row, looking like sentinels on duty, safeguarding all who moved in their shadows. Puffy white clouds weaved along the top peaks, creating a sheer downy blanket of added beauty.

Bringing her gaze closer to Beau's home, she took in trees of all shapes and sizes lining the lane between the church and Charity House's front door. The afternoon breeze swirled fallen leaves into a tapestry of shifting shapes and rich colors of autumn.

Switching to the window on her right, Bella eyed the yard that connected the church to Charity House. The children were at play again. Now that the drama of Ethan's injury was hours old, the fun had resumed.

Some of the more active boys played a hearty game of tag. Others climbed trees. Some of the girls sat in a small group, tying miniature bonnets on their dolls' heads. All in all, the children looked healthy, happy, and well-cared for.

But Bella had seen the anguish in their eyes, the sense of aloneness that they all shared. She had seen the look that both connected them to one another and yet kept them painfully separate. There was an underlying sense of dishonor and disconnection that they didn't think anyone else could understand.

Oh, but Bella understood all too well. She knew the loneliness that was brought on by shame, the inability to connect to people she'd once adored. Even her brother seemed a foreigner to her now. He was too much a man of Christian integrity. Surely he would see through her facade if she allowed him to look too closely. So she wouldn't allow him to look. Ever.

The sound of approaching footsteps halted her thoughts. The hint of authority in the steps told her Beau had returned for round three of their argument.

Bella took a fortifying pull of air into her lungs as her brother joined her.

She pointed to his wrinkled forehead. "If you don't watch out, that line will become permanent."

His scowl deepened. "You can't seriously be considering Shane's offer."

Bella scrunched her face in an identical expression and tried to ignore the fact that her brother looked well. The brute. Happy, too. The hint of contentment in his gold eyes belied his abrupt words with her, as though his shock and anger could do nothing to dispel the joy that was a part of his life, a part of who he was in Christ.

Why did Beau have to be so…*good?*

"Help me to understand, Bella." He scratched his chin in frustration. "Why do you want to do this? And why now?"

She didn't like his tone, but it was the familiar clenched jaw and narrowed eyes that had her bristling. It was the same expression all her brothers gave her when they were about to lecture her over some serious—in their mind only—offense.

Well, she might be the youngest of six. *And* the only

female. But she wasn't a child anymore. "Beauregard O'Toole, you might be older by nine years, and you might have an education from a renowned university and equally impressive seminary, but that does not make you an expert on everything."

"I don't need to be an expert to know you aren't a trained nurse. And, I might also point out, that whine in your voice makes you sound twelve. Hardly the way to go about convincing me of your maturity."

"Don't be so dramatic."

"Me?"

She made a face at him. "Dr. Shane only needs me on a temporary basis. He's not even paying me."

"He's what?"

"Oh, he offered," she said, careful to keep her voice from quivering. "But I refused to hear of it. I don't need the money."

Which had only been a portion of the reason for her refusing the man's offer of a salary. The true reason had been connected to her sense of shame, her sin. Perhaps by volunteering her services for free she could do penance for her blunder with William.

William. So much regret there. Such humiliation. Even now, a month after their disastrous last meeting, she inwardly recoiled at how far she'd walked away from her Christian upbringing. How close she'd come to destroying a family.

How had she been so foolish?

Lord, how do I get past this? How do I make atonement?

Beau touched her arm. "Bella, what aren't you telling me?"

She lowered her gaze. What would he think if he knew the real reason she'd fled London? "Beau, don't. Please don't ask."

Thankfully, Hannah, Beau's wife, walked into the room with the sort of grace any lead actress would envy. Even knowing of her renown, Bella was a little awestruck at the woman's mere presence. She was... stunning. Unforgettable.

It was no wonder she had earned enough prominence on the stage and consequently sufficient money to walk away a wealthy woman after only five years of treading the boards.

With a swoop, her startling green gaze landed on her husband for only a second before swiveling back to Bella. "Beauregard, introduce me to your sister."

He blew out a frustrated breath, but then walked over to his wife and covered her hands with his. For a brief moment, the two shared a connection that went beyond words, similar to the one Bella had seen pass between Trey and Katherine Scott.

And similar to the Scotts, these two were not only in love they actually seemed to like each other. Bella had never thought marriage could include both love and affection, at least not outside her parents' marriage. She'd always assumed Patience and Reginald O'Toole had been lucky.

Luckier, at least, than she would ever be.

Perhaps that was why she had been so willing to

believe William's lies. To convince herself what they had was love. Oh, there had been happiness between them, but also an inexplicable awkwardness. Pain, but hope, as well. But there had never truly been ease between them. And certainly nothing warm.

She'd never realized that until now.

And she felt more the fool because of it.

Smiling, Beau kissed his wife on the nose then turned back to Bella. Unfortunately, his worried scowl returned as soon as he spoke again. "Hannah, I would like you to meet Isabella Constance O'Toole, my baby sister."

"*Younger* sister," Bella corrected.

Hannah gave her a serene smile. Could anyone look lovelier? She was outwardly beautiful, yes, with her waterfall of raven curls, creamy skin and big green eyes, but this woman also had an internal light that was impossible to miss. The Spirit dwelling within her made her radiant. And like Katherine Scott, Hannah had no qualms over tugging Bella into a tight embrace.

Panic gnawed at her but Bella tried not to struggle free.

Why were the women connected with Charity House so kind? So understanding?

Bella wanted to hate them both. She *needed* to hate them both. For their inner goodness, if nothing else. In stark comparison to Hannah and Katherine, Bella felt dirty.

And yet, she yearned. Yearned for something she'd never had in her life. She yearned for sisters.

As though reading her mind, Hannah whispered in her ear. "Welcome, sister."

Bella forced down a sob and tried to pull away.

Hannah's grip tightened. "Whatever pain you're running from, I pray we can offer you a safe haven in which to heal."

Bella quit fighting.

How did Hannah know of her troubles? Had Beau used his preacher eyes to see into her sin and thus alerted his wife?

As ridiculous as the notion seemed, Bella pulled away from Hannah to check for sure. Looking into the other woman's uncomplicated gaze, Bella realized Beau had said nothing. Hannah knew Bella had been scarred because Hannah was a woman.

And just like that, Bella had a sister.

The next morning, a vicious wind thrashed off the mountains in bone-chilling gusts. Shane hunched his shoulders against the driving cold and hurried down Market Street toward the rented rooms that housed his medical practice.

A sharp gust kicked up, whipping Shane's coat tightly around him. Blowing into his cupped palms, he quickened his pace.

Autumn mornings like these, when the temperature dropped, reminded him that living in Colorado came with a cost. Given the alternative, Shane was comfortable with his choice.

Squinting toward the ground, he maneuvered around piles of frozen mud and crossed the threshold of 35 Market Street.

With a solid yank, he shut the door behind him. Warm air enveloped him at once, while outside the wind battered angry fists against the building.

As he waited for his eyes to adjust to the inky stillness of the room, Shane took a deep breath. The sharp scent of iodine filled his lungs. He was in his world now, a world of medicine and science, his personal sanctum of healing.

His vision cleared at last, and he moved farther into the room. With each step his heels clicked across the wooden floor, the sound echoing off the walls. The weak morning sun speared thin fingers of light along his path, providing enough illumination for Shane to work.

Preparing for a long day of visitations, he opened his portable medical bag and took a quick accounting of his supplies. Setting aside the heating iron and tourniquet, he checked the number of sponges and plasters. As he expected after Ethan's accident, Shane was low on bandages. He would order more from the medical supplier in New Brunswick.

Satisfied with his inventory, he replaced the instruments he'd cleaned last night into the small surgery box that was housed inside the larger bag. Stethoscope, scissors, lance, forceps and cutting knife. All necessary tools of his trade.

Clasping the bag shut, Shane circled his gaze around his domain. The room was small, sparse, but serviceable enough.

One day, God willing, he would expand to a larger building.

For now, he had the basics.

A long table positioned in the middle of the room cut his realm in half. Shelves containing books and vials of medicines in powder, liquid and pill form lined the south wall. Two cots sat empty on the north end of the room. The linens would need changing, the wool blankets and pillows airing out. A simple enough task for his new assistant.

His. New. Assistant. The thought made him smile.

Isabella. Constance. O'Toole. The name made him pause.

Shane let out a breath. A very heavy breath.

What had possessed him to hire Bella O'Toole, the sister of a trusted friend?

Evidently, the woman had scrambled his brains. What else explained his trip into insanity? Of course, in his own defense, he'd been awed by her resolve and her undeniable strength under pressure.

Did that mean she belonged in his world, even on a temporary basis?

Yesterday, he'd thought so.

Hadn't he seen past the dazzling beauty, straight to the vulnerable woman underneath?

One thing was certain, Bella O'Toole was a contradiction of strength and innocence. She was also, undoubtedly, hiding a terrible secret.

She'd probably end up more trouble than she was worth.

That thought brought on a painful memory of another woman. His mother—long since dead—was never far from his mind, even after all these years.

Shane tried to suppress the unwanted memories, but they prodded and poked at him, making him feel as helpless and vulnerable as he had at sixteen.

His mother had lived a wretched life, her painful last years the worst. Amanda Bartlett had chosen to become the adored mistress of a wealthy New York businessman. At first, there had been flowers, candy and lots of money. But when Peter Ford's visits ceased, Shane had been forced to watch his once-glorious mother shrink into a sick, embittered, hopeless shell of a woman. And when the money and all hope had run out, he'd been forced to watch her die.

As Shane had held her lifeless body in his young arms, he had vowed to seek revenge on the man responsible. He'd never fully succeeded. And when Ford had failed to father another son, Shane had thrown the scoundrel's offer of legitimacy back in his face and had come to Denver to practice medicine.

What had started as revenge had turned into important work, a calling direct from God. If nothing else, Shane was in a position to prevent women like his mother from dying without a decent chance to beat their illness.

And now, Bella O'Toole, with her secretive eyes and hidden pain, had agreed to stand by his side.

A relieved sigh shuddered through him.

God had brought an answer to his prayers in the form of an unlikely vessel.

Of course, Miss O'Toole hadn't seen all of his patients, nor where they lived. Today would be her first real test.

Eager to get started, Shane finished organizing his supplies and left his office without a backward glance.

Once outside, the cold air frosted his breath and he tightened his coat at the collar. At this time of morning, the streets were relatively deserted. The only sound came from the squeak of a milk wagon's wheels muted in the stiff ruts of the weathered road. He looked to the sky, took a moment to watch the clouds collide into one another in an aggressive, almost hostile manner.

Denver was a world apart from the dingy neighborhood of his youth. Shane didn't live in an especially nice part of the mile-high town, yet even here, one block off a continuous row of brothels and saloons, the filth seemed cleaner than it had on the streets of New York City.

Setting out toward Charity House, Shane lifted his head and instantly realized he wasn't alone on the wooden-slatted sidewalk. A tall figure strode in his direction, bearing down hard. And with each purposeful step, Beauregard O'Toole looked less like a compassionate preacher and more an overprotective big brother.

His face scrunched into a frown, Beau stopped a scarce two feet in front of Shane. His jaw was set at a rock-hard angle as he said, "Just the man I came to see."

Shane couldn't fault the hard tone. If Miss O'Toole had been his own sister he'd feel the same urge to protect.

"Beau." Shane nodded, bracing for the fight that was riding between them on the pounding wind. "I don't need to guess why you're here."

The wind shifted, crashed over them.

Both men held their ground.

"Bella can *not* be your assistant."

Shane's breath turned hot in his lungs. The monumental consequences of losing her so soon struck him like a blow to his gut, hitting like a heavy, leaden weight. "Did she send you to say that?"

"I sent myself. In spite of my arguments, she's bent on this new direction in her life." The frustration in the man's eyes confirmed the truth of his words. "Since she's stubborn as a mule, you need to be the clear thinker here."

"I see." Shane tried to keep his tone mild, but his answer sounded a little too gleeful, even over the howling blasts of air. He erased all emotion from his expression and added, "Perhaps we should have this discussion out of the cold."

Beau gave him a long look before nodding in agreement. "Lead the way."

Neither spoke as Shane retraced his steps and unlocked the door to his office.

He directed Beau to enter ahead of him.

The set of the other man's jaw alerted Shane that the conversation was far from over. Absently, he shoved at his hair. Frustration. Guilt. He didn't have room for either.

Nevertheless, he would hear his friend out. They had a history of working well together. While Shane attended to a patient's physical health, Beau ministered to the spiritual. With God guiding their hands and words, they made a powerful team.

Circling the room, Beau paused to scrub a hand over his face. "You can't hire Bella," he repeated through clenched teeth. "She's not a nurse. She's an opera singer."

Shane bristled. He found himself caught between defending his decision and honoring his friendship with this man. "According to your sister, she has taken a self-imposed sabbatical."

Beau rolled his shoulders, then sighed. "There's more to the story. Something's wrong. I don't like that she showed up, tight-lipped and unannounced."

Ah. Miss O'Toole had yet to explain herself to her brother. Oddly enough, Shane wasn't surprised. "And that's your only concern? That she's hiding something from you?"

Closing his eyes, Beau shook his head. "You have to understand, Bella isn't like most women."

Remembering the courage she'd displayed with Ethan, the compassion in her manner, the instant display of rebellion when Beau had first shown up, Shane gave an ironic lift of his eyebrows. "Well, that certainly needed clearing up."

Beau's lips twitched but instead of responding right away, he walked to a row of books and ran a finger along the spines.

Shane gauged the mood in the room and decided on a tactic. The brother might not hear his words, but surely the preacher would. "I remember you telling me once that if a man waits to be certain of a course of action, he's sure to be too late. Those were your exact words. I know. I wrote them down."

Beau's shoulders stiffened before he spun on his heel to glare at Shane. "I was referring to God's Will for *your* life."

Shane allowed himself a tight smile of satisfaction. "Precisely."

Beau crossed his arms over his chest. Genuine concern fell across his face. "Bella has never lived in the real world. Her whole life has been about make-believe and fantasy. She doesn't understand anything outside the theater."

Studying his friend's expression closely, Shane leaned a shoulder against the wall. Again, he appealed to the preacher and not the brother. "The most unlikely people can demonstrate courage. And given her lack of experience, perhaps it's time Miss O'Toole left the opera for a while."

"Don't misunderstand me. I'm glad she's left. In fact, I'm relieved. At least, in theory." Beau started pacing through the room, slapping a fist against his thigh as he walked. "We both know the perils of *that* life."

Shane nodded gravely. The Denver brothels were filled with women who had failed on the stage. Whether due to lack of talent or disappearing youth, far too many women had nowhere else to go and no hope of gaining respectable employment.

"It's whatever drove Bella to leave the opera that worries me," Beau continued. "Something terrible happened to her in London."

Why deny the truth? Shane, too, believed something bad had happened to Miss O'Toole. But instead of concern at the thought, certainty filled him. The woman was meant to be here, in Denver, assisting him instead of singing opera. There was something else happening here, something bigger than any of them understood.

Something from God.

All along, Shane had assumed Miss O'Toole had been led to him by the Lord in order to assist in his practice. But maybe—*maybe*—she'd been brought to Shane for a bigger reason.

One he couldn't comprehend just yet, and probably wasn't supposed to. As Beau often said when he was thinking like a preacher and not a worried brother, it all came down to walking in faith.

"Perhaps this is just what your sister needs," Shane suggested. "A safe environment to spread her wings and—"

"*Safe?*" Beau stopped pacing to glare in Shane's direction. "She'll spend her days in brothels, saloons and mining camps."

Shane took exception. "Places where people are still people. The same places, I might remind you, you and your wife inhabit daily. If Hannah can do it, surely your sister can, as well."

"Hannah's different. She's strong."

"Your sister is strong, too."

"Hannah isn't alone."

"Your sister won't be either." Shane pushed from the wall and stood tall, unbending in his conviction. "*I'll* be with her."

Clearly unimpressed with the bold declaration, Beau turned away and started pacing again, muttering under his breath. "How will she survive once her money runs out?"

Rage shot up, threatened to linger, but Shane squashed it back. "This from you? A preacher well-versed in the Bible? Jesus told his disciples not to worry. 'Look at the birds in the air; they do not sow or reap or store away in barns, and yet your heavenly father feeds them.'"

Eyes blinking in shock, Beau responded with a tiny, rather hapless nod, but Shane continued before the other man could speak. "Rest assured, my friend. This situation is only temporary. And, let's face it, your sister may not make it through the week."

The thought left Shane a little sick, for reasons he refused to explore.

"Oh, she'll last." Beau sank onto a hard-backed, wooden chair and released a frustrated puff of air. "Once Bella gets something in her mind, there's no stopping her."

"Good to know." For a moment, *just one,* Shane allowed his heart to soar with possibilities beyond a simple working relationship. Stunned by the direction of his thoughts, he quickly shut down the notion. "In the meantime, I assure you I plan to continue interviewing qualified candidates."

Beau stared at him for a long, measuring moment. Shane remained unmoving under his friend's scrutiny.

At last, Beau nodded. "Fair enough." Looking far more at ease now, he stretched out his long legs and crossed them at the ankles. "What's on your schedule today?"

"I'll be making visitations all afternoon," Shane said.

Beau leaned forward and rested his elbows on his knees. "Is Lizzie one of those…visitations?"

"Of course. After I retrieve your sister, Mattie's brothel will be our first stop."

"Is that a fact?" A twinkle of amusement entered Beau's eyes. "Do you expect Mattie to show up during said visit?"

Shane grinned at last. "When doesn't the woman make her presence known, dramatic entrance and all?"

"Dr. Bartlett, I believe I owe you an apology." A slow grin spread across the preacher's lips. "Clearly, I underestimated you."

"You aren't the first."

"Bella won't know what hit her."

"That is the general idea."

Beau pushed out of the chair and walked over to slap Shane on the back. "You are either very brave, my friend, or very, *very* stupid."

Shane's smile disappeared. "Maybe both."

Beau chuckled. "Time will tell."

And that, Shane thought, was exactly what he feared most.

Chapter Five

Before the sun had fully risen, Bella faced her first dilemma of the day. She had no idea what a nurse wore while attending patients. If her experience with Ethan Scott was any indication, the work would be messy.

That meant silk was out. Satin, too. Definitely no ruffles or lace.

A quick rummage through her trunks sent a wave of distress rippling through her. Sighing, Bella rubbed a finger across her temple. Maybe she should have thought this through better.

She had nothing appropriate to wear. Which only made her more convicted to pursue this new course for her life. As her mother always said, "If it comes too easy, it's simply not worth doing."

Perhaps her new sister-in-law would have a solution.

Shoving her feet into slippers, Bella wrapped her dressing gown tightly around her and went in search of Hannah.

Out in the hallway, her gaze tracked everywhere, past the wallpaper, the rugs, the wood floors underneath, the lone chair halfway down the corridor. Nothing looked familiar. Bella spun to her left and then to her right.

She couldn't seem to get her bearings.

Beau's house wasn't all that large but it wasn't small either. Hannah had given her a tour of the home last night. Navigating the two stories had seemed easy enough. But this morning, Bella was hopelessly lost. Understandable, she supposed. She'd only spent a handful of days in a real home. Her childhood had consisted of makeshift beds either backstage or in a temporary flat.

Focus, Bella. Focus.

Choosing a direction at random, she set out. She hadn't gone far when she stopped midstep and inhaled deeply.

The smells.

Yes, the smells were different here. Clove, cinnamon, coffee, the lingering scent of food mixed with lemon oil. It was all so very pleasant. So heartwarming. A slice of the kind of life she'd secretly dreamed of and only now just realized how much.

A deep longing for something—something *more*—rose up, threatened to linger, but she fought the disturbing emotion back with a hard swallow.

William's necklace weighed heavy around her neck, a bold reminder that she'd failed her first real test as a woman. The urge to yank off the offensive talisman burned, but she would not touch the necklace. She would *not*.

Needing to think a moment, Bella collapsed against the wall and closed her eyes. Pure and simple, she was a fraud. She was no more a nurse than she was a pure-hearted woman.

Yet no one need know of her deception, did they? She was a trained performer, after all, schooled from child-hood to take on varied roles. How hard could it be to pretend innocence?

The key, of course, would be to keep her mouth shut. Little talking meant few revelations. Yes, yes, that was it. *Silence.*

Mouth pressed in a firm line, she fumbled from the wall, and resumed her search for the perfect dress to wear on this first day of her atoning.

The sound of—was that retching?—stopped her cold. Bella spun on her heel.

"Hannah?"

There was a pause, followed by a series of coughs and sniffles. "We're in here," came a weak voice.

Bella rushed in the direction of the voice. When she got to the end of the hall, she halted at the sight of her sister-in-law crumbled on the floor of the washroom, her head pressed in the lap of a tiny, unusual-looking old woman.

Mavis. This had to be Hannah's adopted grandmother.

Bella thought Beau had been exaggerating when he'd told her about the woman. But Mavis's hair was indeed white as fresh-fallen snow and it did shoot out in wild waves from every direction. Her age was indetermi-nate, and her clothing bright. A bawdy old girl, as

Bella's brother Tyler would call her. Unconventional in every way. And long past the days of innocence.

No wonder Hannah adored the woman.

And it was obvious Mavis loved Hannah in return.

Her thin, gnarled fingers petted Hannah's head in slow, gentle strokes. "Deep breaths, baby girl." Her voice was as hard and raspy as Beau had described. "It'll pass."

From her seat on the floor, Mavis looked up at Bella and grinned. "Don't take no brains to tell you're Pastor Beau's sister."

Waving a limp hand in Bella's general direction, Hannah took a shaky breath. "Bella, meet Mavis. Mavis, Bella."

Casting the older woman a quick nod of acknowledgment, Bella dropped to her knees and lifted Hannah's tangled mass of ebony curls. "What can I do to help you?"

Hannah lifted her head, dropped it just as quickly. "Don't look so frightened, Bella dear." She swiped the back of her hand across her mouth and struggled to sit up. "I'm fine now, really."

Clearly, Hannah exaggerated. The edges around her mouth were pulled tight with tension and her face was leached of color.

Bella exchanged a concerned glance with Mavis. "You don't look fine," she said for them both.

"I will be in a moment." She took several slow, full gulps of air. "It'll pass. Once the baby grows bigger."

Bella shifted her weight from her knees to her heels.

The very edge of excitement and fear had her rocking back and forth. "How long has this been going on?"

"A few days now." Hannah grinned in spite of her misery. But then her eyes glazed over and she bent over herself.

Mavis lifted the pot by her feet just in time.

Hannah finished with a series of dry heaves.

"Lay your head back down in my lap," Mavis ordered, gently pulling until Hannah obeyed the command.

Once settled again, Hannah's hair fell forward, curtaining half her face.

Unsure how to proceed, Bella asked, "Does Beau know yet?"

Surely he would have told Bella. Wouldn't he? Maybe not. He'd been awfully angry with her when he'd gone to bed last night.

"I wanted to make sure before I told him," Hannah said.

Bella felt very young and very inexperienced, but if she was going to work as a doctor's assistant she better know such things. "How...how do you make sure?"

With a shaky hand, Hannah shoved the hair off her face, glanced at the full bedpan near Mavis's crossed feet. "I think it's safe to say God has blessed us with child."

"Oh, Hannah. I'm so happy for you."

Bella reached out and smoothed her fingers across her sister-in-law's forehead. She wanted to connect with this woman, to become her friend, as well as her sister, but something in Bella refused to soften, something dark warned her to keep her distance. "When is the blessed day?" she asked in a whisper.

"In about seven months."

Seven months. So soon. So far away.

"Will you tell Beau soon?"

A smile played at the edges of Hannah's lips. "As soon as he returns from his errand in town."

"He'll be pleased," Mavis announced, lifting her chin to a jaunty, I-know-these-things angle.

"Yes. Yes, he will." Hannah sat up again, blinked several times. Slowly, the color returned to her cheeks.

Bella sighed at the sight of Beau's pregnant wife. Bittersweet tears welled in her own eyes. She dashed them away with a single swipe. But, truthfully, she'd rarely seen such a look of contentment on another woman's face, had never thought such joy possible.

Surely, she wasn't jealous was she?

"This is truly a blessing from God," Mavis said with such conviction, Bella gave the older woman a closer inspection. She didn't look like a believing Christian. In truth, she had the hard, craggy exterior of someone who had lived a difficult life.

Ah, but Bella had already learned a person's exterior was no indication of the inner heart.

"It is a blessing." Hannah squeezed Mavis's hand. "And I pray, God willing, our child looks just like my husband."

Bella sighed again. No matter which parent it took after, the child would be beautiful. And not to mention he, *or she,* would be the first grandchild in the O'Toole family.

Bella's parents would want to know the happy news. They would want to be present for the child's birth.

And if Bella was still living in Denver, there would be questions. More like a full-blown interrogation.

Oh, no. No, no, no. Bella could bear anything but one of her mother's "concerned" lectures, the ones that always began with, "If you would have listened to me in the first place."

That settled it, then. Bella would be long departed before her parents arrived. She had less than seven months to figure out her next step.

When the time came, she'd be glad to go. She bit down on her lip.

Wouldn't she?

Why did she feel the loss already? Why did she sense leaving this place, this town, *these people* would bring on far more regret than anything she'd left behind in London?

Shane waited for his new assistant in the O'Toole's front parlor. A quick glance around the tiny room revealed Hannah's handiwork. She'd decorated with an overabundance of frills and lace. But instead of feeling too feminine, the fancy decor created a warm, comforting sense of home.

At ten, he'd tried to create something similar for his mother. But his efforts had been pitiful, a small lace doily the only thing he could afford to give his mother the day she'd turned thirty, the first of many birthdays Peter Ford had missed.

Forcing down a surge of restlessness, Shane took another, slower study of the room. Framed photographs of the famous O'Tooles covered all four green walls.

Playbills, clippings and newspaper reviews filled two entire tables, all clear evidence that Beau and Hannah O'Toole cared deeply for their relatives.

What would it be like, Shane wondered, to be a member of such a large and loving family?

A dark, wistful longing he hadn't experienced since childhood speared through his heart, leaving a vague sense of dissatisfaction. Disgusted with himself—*with the unexpected emotion*—Shane remained very still and forced his mind clear.

He had no room in his life for dreams abandoned years ago. His patients depended on his sole dedication to the science of medicine. Logic, reason and hard work, yes, those were the three fundamentals of his life.

The distant sound of light, airy footsteps hailed Miss O'Toole's impending entrance. Shane shook himself out of his troubled musings. By the time his assistant joined him, he had successfully buried all thought, save one. They had a busy day ahead of them.

"Here I am," she said in her lilting accent, her arms outstretched as if to present herself for his inspection.

Turning slightly, Shane brought his gaze in direct line with Bella O'Toole. His eyes loitered on her face. *So many secrets buried in that beautiful head.*

The thought did nothing to ease his foul mood.

Pulling her bottom lip between her teeth, she lowered her hands to her hips. "Are you ready to begin our new alliance?"

New alliance? A swelling of something he couldn't

quite identify streamed through his resolve to think logically. Was it doubt? Or something more complex?

Needing a moment to collect his thoughts, Shane studied Miss O'Toole's chosen ensemble for the day. She'd dressed in a simple blue dress, rather nondescript, but she'd covered it with a bright purple apron with red patches sewn haphazardly across the hem. The dress alone was acceptable enough, but the apron added an entirely different quality to the overall look, bordering on the ugly.

He did a quick estimate of Miss O'Toole's height and weight and figured she'd borrowed the two garments from Mavis Tierney. No wonder the dress and apron clashed so completely.

Suppressing a grin, Shane moved his gaze back to Miss O'Toole's face.

She wore her hair down, the golden locks cascading in a riot of curls down her back. She'd pulled the thick mane off her face with a black ribbon, tied with a large bow on top. She should look silly.

She looked…incredible.

Rendered momentarily speechless, Shane lowered his gaze for a final pass, and stopped dead at her shoes, or rather her fancy, thin-heeled *slippers*.

His brows dived into a scowl. "Those won't do."

He hadn't realized how harsh his tone sounded until her eyes widened in response. She looked shocked, offended perhaps, but she quickly covered the emotion with a pleasant, almost vacant look in her eyes. "Well, they're all I have."

Her flat tone gave nothing away, nor did her eyes.

How could the woman hide her thoughts so quickly and so completely? He puzzled over the question until he remembered she was a trained actress, an opera singer of the first order who made her living pretending to be someone she was not.

Like any man dealing with a woman he didn't understand, Shane took a fortifying breath and prepared for the inevitable battle ahead.

"We'll take care of finding you appropriate footwear in town," he said, using his mildest tone in hopes of forestalling any argument on her part. "We'll get you a pair of shoes that will be warmer and more comfortable and—"

"Whatever you say."

"—better suited for trekking through ice and mud."

Whatever you say? He blinked.

"Did you just agree with me, Miss O'Toole?"

Tucking a loose strand of hair beneath the black ribbon, she lifted a careless shoulder. "You would know better than I what sort of shoes I should wear."

And just like that, she threw him off balance. *Again.* This time with her complete cooperation. Would this woman never stop surprising him?

"Right, then." He cleared the shock out of his voice and turned all business. "Let's be off."

Feeling more hopeful than he had in months, Shane helped Miss O'Toole with her coat and then stepped back while she tugged on the matching hat and gloves.

Once outside, Shane gripped her elbow carefully and assisted her into his small, but serviceable buggy.

She wiggled and shifted and squirmed until she finally settled herself on the cushioned seat. Only then did she turn her head and smile down at him.

Shane's pulse kicked hard in his chest. The sight of all that beauty aimed solely at him was like a swift punch to his gut.

He quickly broke eye contact and made his way to the other side of the carriage and climbed aboard. With mechanical movements, he snapped the reins and clicked his tongue.

His horse set out at a slow, easy gait.

Focused on the passing scenery, Miss O'Toole remained silent during the ride into town. Shane took the opportunity to slip covert glances in her direction. Her wool coat was the color of a Colorado pine and set off her creamy skin to perfection. With her honey, sun-kissed curls pouring past her shoulders she looked almost imaginary. A storybook princess brought to life.

But she was real. Very real. Her scent gave her away. She smelled of sweet perfume, like fresh jasmine, all pleasant and inviting.

Shane smiled.

Without warning, she turned her head, and Shane found his lips slipping into a frown. Imprisoned in those remarkable tawny eyes the dark, wistful longing he'd experienced in the parlor returned, somehow stronger, and with enough force to yank the breath out of his lungs.

He tightened his hands on the reins and forced his at-

tention back to the road. It took every ounce of his will-
power not to look at her again.

You do not need this sort of trouble, he warned himself.
It's dangerous, imprudent and reckless. Very reckless.

Then again…

Perhaps Shane was thinking too hard, allowing a
pretty face to complicate a simple matter. Perhaps all he
needed was a little distance from the woman sitting
entirely too close to him.

With that in mind, he turned his thoughts to the day's
schedule and scrutinized the road with careful attention.

The rhythmic turning of the wheels mingling with his
horse's steady gait hypnotized him until Shane had no idea
how much time elapsed. Surely, no more than ten minutes.

At last, he drew the carriage to a stop in the alleyway
between Mattie's brothel and the Smoking Horse Saloon.

This was it, their first real test as doctor and temporary assistant.

He let out a slow breath of tension, shoved his fingers
through his hair and tugged at the ends.

In a matter of minutes, Shane would discover what
Miss O'Toole was actually made of. And for both their
sakes, as well as his patients', he prayed she was up for
the tasks that lay ahead.

Chapter Six

Truly? Bella squinted into the muted, gray light. He'd *truly* brought her to a filthy, stinky, back alley in the heart of a derelict part of town?

There had to be some mistake.

Why would the man direct them straight to a dead end and simply sit there without speaking?

Swallowing her confusion, Bella covered her nose against the stench of garbage and stale liquor. She shot her gaze in all directions. Unfortunately, the jagged rooftops swallowed the sunlight and blue sky above, casting dark, ominous shadows over them. She could only make out a scant few details such as dirt, dirt and, oh, right, *more dirt*.

Confusion giving way to frustration, she glanced at the good doctor for some clue to this unusual turn of events. He simply stared at her. Blinking, staring, grinning, frowning? She couldn't tell. Shadows, long and deep, concealed his features entirely.

Well, of course. Why make this easy for her?

In spite of a hot surge of rebellion, Bella scooted a little closer to the man, casting her gaze to the right and back to the left again. She didn't particularly like the dark.

And, uh, were the walls closing in on them by chance?

Stifling a gasp, Bella quickly lowered her gaze to the ground that…was…*moving.*

Moving?

One explanation came to mind.

Rats.

In spite of the calm horse at the end of the reins and the equally calm man beside her, the street was teaming with hideous rodents, their sharp little fang teeth waiting for a fresh ankle to bite.

She tried to pretend she was on the stage with a packed audience. She failed. And all at once Bella surrendered to abject terror. "Do…do you see that?" She jabbed her finger toward the ground.

"See what?"

"R…r-r-r…r-r-r-rats! Everywhere." She clawed at his sleeve. She hated rats worse than the dark.

He gave her hand a condescending pat. "They're more afraid of you than you are of them. Give it a moment more and they'll scurry away."

"No. You…you…you d-d-don't understand." She yanked hard on his arm, pulling at him until his ear came close enough for her to speak in a loud whisper. "I hate rats!"

One by one, he slowly untangled her fingers from his sleeve and chuckled. "I should think you've seen enough of the little black creatures in your life. Aren't they a staple backstage of most theaters?"

The man had a point, a rather large point. But Bella was not in the mood to concede anything to the unfeeling, overly calm beast. "Ssss…So?"

"So," he said with the same practiced patience he'd used on Ethan yesterday. "I should think you've had plenty of time to get over any phobia you might have incurred through the years. You must know they won't hurt you."

They won't hurt you? Was the man insane? "Rats bite."

"Has one bitten you before?" he asked, his voice filled with genuine worry.

Oh, right, *now* he showed concern. When it was too, too late.

Bella jerked her chin. "That is not the point."

"Has a rat bitten you in the past?" he asked again, his tone growing softer and his hand patting with less condescension.

"*No.* But, at the risk of stating the obvious, I…I…I am wearing slippers."

"Right. I forgot." The man sounded entirely too passive, almost gleeful in the face of her panic.

Something bigger was going on here, bigger than rat teeth searching for Bella flesh. And just like that, she knew. Beau's terribly important meeting this morning made perfect sense now.

This little trip down rat alley was a test.

One the horse was passing, one the doctor was passing and one Bella had every intention of passing, as well.

Just give her a moment.

Once she started breathing again she'd have her fear under control. Oh, sure, her hands were shaking uncontrollably. And her heart was pounding a fast tempo against her ribs. But she would not submit easily.

Lord, empower me with the courage to do Your work today, regardless of the black furry challenges You've set before me.

"While we're waiting for our new friends to find a hiding place," Dr. Shane began in a matter-of-fact tone, "I should take this opportunity to warn you about what's to come."

"Of course," she said, waiting silently for him to proceed. *Anything* to get her mind off sharp, pointy fangs.

Turning her head slightly, she considered the doctor more carefully now that her eyes were adjusting to the shadows. In the dim light, his features had taken on a series of sharp angles and well-defined planes. His eyes were the color of polished pewter.

Unfortunately, the look he cast her was completely impersonal, as though he'd slid an invisible shutter across his features.

Bella swallowed a sudden urge to cry. She wished she could understand what was going on in that complicated mind of his.

"Our first patient is Lizzie." He shifted away from her and set the brake. "She's suffering from consumption, as many of her kind do." The sorrow in his eyes told her there was more to the story than he was revealing.

"Her kind?" she asked.

His head rotated back in her direction. An inner

struggle was written across his face. "Prostitutes. Lizzie earns her living by accepting favors from men."

A gust of cold, misty air swept through the alley at his proclamation. Bella shivered.

"We're at a brothel?" she asked, trying to hide her terrible fascination at the notion.

"Yes."

Bella studied the two buildings on either side of her, silently wondering which establishment was their destination.

As though sensing her unspoken question, Dr. Shane pointed to his left. "It's that one."

Cocking her head in fierce concentration, she eyed the sooty brick and mortar. "I see."

She felt rather than saw him take a deep breath. "You are not shocked?"

"Of course not."

Well, maybe a little. But she pitched her voice to a confident level. "I *am* a woman of the world, after all. In fact, I have sung the lead in the opera *La Traviata*."

She hoped her rapid blinking didn't belie her bold words. She might have sung the notes of a doomed prostitute, but she'd never fully understood the tragic Camille's choices. Her performance had suffered, resulting in the worst reviews of her life.

"Did you enjoy playing the ill-fated courtesan?"

"The story was quite sad," she said. Then sighed. "I always wished she'd have accepted her young suitor's love and simply left…" She cleared her throat. "That life."

That life.

The very same life William had offered her.

Of its own volition, her hand reached for the locket around her neck. She spread her fingers across her collarbone and let out another sigh. If she was honest with herself, she'd admit she'd left London out of fear, not moral conviction. Eventually, she'd have given in to William's vows of love, just as the fictional Camille had done over and over again with her various suitors.

Bella hadn't believed in her own inner strength, hadn't believed she had the character to turn away from her temptation and the sin that came with it.

So she'd run.

She was still running.

"Brace yourself, Miss O'Toole. The play glosses over the harsh reality of a woman dying of consumption."

She tossed her head back and scoffed at him. "You needn't worry about me. I've seen my share of ugliness in the world. I will not be shocked."

Oh, but she would be. She was sure of it, yet not for the obvious reasons. She sensed, down to the bottom of her slippers, that she would find a kindred spirit in Lizzie, the prostitute.

And that, Bella thought miserably, told the true state of her wretched sinner's soul.

Stepping quickly to the ground, Shane studied the area surrounding his feet. Confident the last remaining rat had fled, he proceeded to Miss O'Toole's side of the carriage.

"Ready to start our day?" he asked in what he hoped

was a pleasant enough voice, one that would soothe away the majority of her fears.

At her wide-eyed stare, a thread of discomfort wiggled through his conscience. Perhaps he should have brought her to the front door after all. Perhaps his scheme to toss her immediately into the thick of things wasn't as well-thought out as he'd told himself.

Unfortunately, it was too late for second guesses. What was done was done. He'd simply have to do his best to protect her from this point forward.

Inching toward the edge of her seat, she squeezed her eyes shut a moment then said, "I suppose I'm as ready as I'll ever be."

Shane stifled a smile at the muffled squeak in her voice, the one she was trying so hard to hide behind a brilliant smile.

Oh, she was a brave one. He'd give her that.

In spite of the fact that her eyes brimmed with mistrust and she glared at the ground around his feet, Shane knew Miss O'Toole would exit the buggy. Eventually.

He wished she'd lift her head and look at him, though. She would only make herself miserable if she continued searching for rats—especially since there was a high possibility she'd find one. Or twelve.

Well, rodents or not, they had a schedule to keep.

Stretching out his hand, he waited patiently for her to gather her courage.

Still glaring at his feet, she took a fortifying breath, boldly placed her palm into his and finally looked him directly in the eye.

An unmistakable scratching noise filled the silence. Her face drained of color.

He opened his mouth to make some inane comment about nothing to fear, he would protect her from the big bad rats, but words failed him. "I…" He broke off, wrapped his hand tighter around hers and gave an encouraging squeeze.

She gripped him back with equal intensity.

He should release her. No doubt about it. And yet, Shane clutched her fingers as though she was the most important thing ever to come across his path.

Lord, what's happening here?

Struggling for air, he drew her slowly to the ground. Only after she found her balance did he release her hand.

This was going to be one very long day.

"After you," he said.

"Right."

To his amusement, she set out at a slow, careful pace, tiptoeing as though she could escape notice one baby step at a time. He allowed a slow smile to spread across his lips.

The woman was anything but dull.

And her rat phobia was oddly charming.

Still grinning at Miss O'Toole's wretched attempt to avoid detection, Shane lifted his medical bag and took off after her.

Thankfully, no furry creature dared tread in their path thus far. Pulling alongside her, Shane gripped Miss O'Toole's elbow and led her to the backdoor of the brothel.

With each step he silently reviewed the prescribed

plan in his mind. In spite of his previous doubts, he knew it was important to stay the course this morning. Everyone, especially their patients, depended on Miss O'Toole fulfilling her appointed duties without hesitation just as she'd done yesterday with Ethan.

No matter what they came across today, Shane would not gloss over any portion of the work that lay ahead. If Miss O'Toole was to remain as his assistant for any length of time, she needed to understand exactly what a brothel looked like from behind the scenes. No false sheen. No glamour. Just the harsh reality of shame and early death.

Standing on the back doorstep, Shane considered his assistant's nervous profile before knocking. Regardless of her "woman of the world" platitudes, she was in for a shock this morning.

But it was Shane who received the biggest surprise when the door swung open and a young woman stared at him from the other side of the threshold.

Two thoughts came to mind. The girl couldn't be more than fifteen, and he'd never seen her before. She was well-dressed, and unbelievably attractive with her brown hair, blue eyes and light brown skin. Even more startling, innocence radiated out of her.

But there could be only one reason for her presence in the brothel at this time of day. She was one of Mattie's newest girls, another casualty of the harsh western frontier.

Which made no sense.

Unlike most madams in the territory, Mattie Silks had her own unique set of standards. She had never hired anyone this young before.

Unaware of his thoughts, the girl's gaze flitted from him to Miss O'Toole and back to him again.

"May I help you?" she asked in a voice just above a squeak, sounding much like Miss O'Toole had when she'd discovered the alley's rodent problem.

Shane stepped forward. "I'm Dr. Bartlett. Would you please inform Miss Silks I have arrived?"

The girl's gaze dropped to the medical bag in his hand. "Oh. Yes, of course."

The relief in her young voice made Shane smile. She was not one of Mattie's girls. Yet.

But how long would that hold true? Had Mattie relaxed her standards for this beautiful child?

Watching the young woman pivot and then walk out of the room with guileless elegance, Shane shuddered at the inevitable tragedy her life would become if something wasn't done soon.

Yet, what could he do?

He would alert Pastor Beau of her existence. Surely, the preacher would know what course of action to take next.

Feeling a bit more hopeful, Shane dragged an unsteady hand through his hair and offered up a silent prayer. *Lord, You are the Great Protector. I pray You keep that young girl from falling into the sin of this house.*

"You don't think she's—" Miss O'Toole let out an audible breath. "You know. A…a…"

"*No.*"

She turned to look at him.

Their gazes locked.

Held.

Held.

"You are sure of this?"

"Completely."

Her brows drew into a delicate frown and she angled her head in confusion. "But how do you know?"

"I know."

Her left eyebrow lifted a fraction closer to her hairline, giving her a slightly wounded look. "You can simply look at someone and know that sort of thing?"

Realizing his answer was important to her, and not quite understanding how he knew or why, he nodded slowly, never taking his eyes off her stricken face. "Sometimes."

"Oh." Her voice came out steady enough, but anguish was written all over her features.

If the question of a young girl's innocence could distress the woman this much, what would happen when she actually followed Shane upstairs and witnessed the ugly realities of life in a brothel?

She thought playing the part of a doomed courtesan gave her an understanding of the world inside these walls. But there was no glamour to be found here.

And suddenly, as sure as he knew his own name, Shane didn't want to subject this fine, Christian woman to the dark world upstairs. Not yet.

In fact, he *never* wanted to watch this bright, young opera singer lose her innocence simply because she agreed to assist him when no one else had the courage or the character.

For some inexplicable reason, Shane desperately

needed Miss O'Toole to keep her fantasies intact. He needed to believe there were people who still had such illusions. And most of all, he needed physical proof that there were people living in this world free of pain, death and complicated life choices.

"Wait for me in the carriage," he said in an unbending tone.

Her face took on the stubborn edge Shane was beginning to recognize. And dread.

"No."

"Miss O'Toole—"

"I will not leave your side before I've had a chance to prove myself. *I will not.*"

Stunned at the relief her words brought him, Shane lifted a hand to her, dropped it just as quickly. This was not about him. "It is for your own good. You shouldn't see—"

"Don't do this. Please. Not now." She placed a gentle, yet firm grip on his arm. "I promise you, I will be quite fine."

And perhaps she would.

But would Shane?

Chapter Seven

Much to her shock and against all effort to the contrary, tears invaded Bella's eyes. She would not buckle under Dr. Shane's misguided attempt to protect her. She would *not*.

Refusing to look at him until she had her emotions under control, Bella called upon the familiar breathing technique she used to calm her nerves. In. Out. In. Out.

In...

Out...

But no matter how slowly she breathed, she could not seem to get her thoughts under control. What if this man could see into her heart and know what was there? Hadn't he said he knew the young girl was innocent? Could he also know Bella was not, at least not in her heart?

Still a bit unsteady, she continued breathing deeply. She was being ridiculous. It didn't matter what Dr. Shane thought of her. God had given her this chance to atone for her sin with William.

The urge to wrap her fingers around the locket came strong, but Bella balled her hand into a tight fist and cast a quick glance at Dr. Shane.

He appeared lost in his own thoughts, looking toward the ceiling with grave interest.

Perhaps he was impatient to begin his day.

Or maybe there was something else on his mind.

Before Bella could contemplate further, the beautiful child returned.

"I am to tell you to proceed directly to Miss Lizzie's room. My..." She let her words trail off, cringing with obvious embarrassment at some unplanned slip of the tongue. "That is, *Miss Silks* said she will join you in a moment."

The doctor nodded. "Thank you, Miss..."

"Annabeth."

His lips cracked into a smile. Warm. Accessible. The man certainly had his share of charm.

"Thank you, Miss Annabeth," he said. "You may tell Mattie that I've set off for Lizzie's room with my new assistant in tow."

Smiling at his choice of words, Bella followed her employer through a pair of swinging doors. She glanced over her shoulder in time to witness Annabeth retreating in the opposite direction.

Bella paused. "I wonder why she isn't at Charity House with other young girls her age."

"That's a question I plan to ask Mattie as soon as the opportunity arises," he ground out.

Understanding his frustration, Bella remained silent as they made their way through the lower level of the brothel.

A sickening dread crept through her stomach but she refused to flinch, not at the hideous decor or the stale odor of cigar smoke mingled with cheap perfume.

In truth, the interior wasn't as bad as she'd expected. It was worse. *Much worse.*

Bella had never seen such an ill-staged setting, not even in her early days of playing smaller, seedier venues. The gaudy red-velvet furniture stood in stark contrast to the gold filigree wallpaper, lamps and tables. A trio of fake-looking Oriental rugs covered the wood flooring. Vulgar paintings hung on the walls, their bold colors and shocking themes made Bella think she was walking inside a cliché.

Really, Miss Silks, must you be so obvious?

More disturbed than she cared to admit, Bella inched closer to the doctor, nearly nipping his heels with her toes.

A winding staircase took them upstairs to a long hallway with five doors along both walls. The carpet on this floor was much shabbier, a floral print long since faded.

There was a sense of neglect up here, as though the madam had spent her time, effort and money decorating the lower level—for what it was worth.

But how had Miss Silks decorated the individual rooms?

Bella had her answer as soon as the doctor opened the third door on their right.

The smell hit her first. Musty, sour, rank. As she

closed the door behind them, she decided she actually missed the rancid back alleyway. Rats and all.

Squinting into the darkened room, she waited for her vision to clear before stepping forward. The ragged curtains and threadbare furnishings brought one word to mind. *Forgotten.*

Dr. Shane set his bag on a chair near the bed and began unbuttoning his coat.

Bella did the same.

"Good morning, Lizzie," he said in a low voice, placing his coat across the foot of the bed.

Setting her coat next to Dr. Shane's, Bella followed his gaze to the shriveled, pale form lying in the large bed in the center of the room.

While the doctor rummaged in his bag, Bella studied the poor woman. It was impossible to determine her age. Her long, black hair hung in dirty tangles and her face was pinched into a grimace of pain.

Much as the downstairs looked like a poorly constructed theater set, Lizzie looked like an actress bent on playing herself yet failing to bring genuine enthusiasm to the role.

A wave of sympathy crested. Bella couldn't take her eyes off the pitiful sight of the worn-out woman.

Unaware of her morbid fascination, Dr. Shane wrapped a stethoscope around his neck and pivoted back to his patient. With practiced movements, he took Lizzie's limp hand in his and pressed two fingers against her wrist. After a minute, he released her and touched her brow.

Riveted, Bella stared at the doctor's fingers as they made a rhythmic sweep across Lizzie's forehead. The elegant gesture reminded Bella of an artist's expert stroke across a canvas.

And yet, it was the compassion in his manner that struck the strongest chord within her. Bella stood in awe. What depth of character he had, to look past the sin and straight into this poor woman's tortured heart.

This man was a true model of Christian integrity.

"How are you feeling today?" he asked his patient.

"Not so good," she croaked.

He patted her hand. "We'll try to make it better."

His tone was so gentle, so patient, Bella nearly wept. She desperately wanted somcone—anyone—*him*—to show her that same careful consideration.

If only she could leave her memories of William behind. Perhaps then…

Then, what?

What did she want from Dr. Shane?

As though sensing her inspection, he turned his gaze to meet hers. But his eyes were filled with an inner sadness, not curiosity.

At the sight of his unguarded despair, Bella's thoughts of herself disappeared. She had a compelling urge to rush to him, to ease his pain somehow.

Just as she moved forward, Lizzie began coughing. Bella switched directions.

Acting on pure instinct, she moved in behind Lizzie and lifted her head to a less awkward angle. "There, now," she soothed. "Take your time."

She continued to speak softly, practically chattering, until she sensed the doctor watching her again.

Compelled by some silent nudge inside her, she lifted her gaze to his and found that his eyes were no longer sad. They were filled with a mixture of surprise and gratitude.

Her breath backed up in her lungs.

No theater review had ever brought such instant pleasure.

Without a word, he handed her a clean handkerchief and cocked his head toward Lizzie. Understanding his silent command, Bella placed the cloth against the woman's lips and wiped.

"You poor dear," she whispered, never taking her eyes off the doctor.

He held her stare, silent a moment, and then stepped forward. "I'll take it from here."

Nodding, Bella lowered Lizzie's head to the pillow and moved out of his way.

He reached out and squeezed her hand as she passed by him. "Thank you."

Choked with emotion, she simply nodded.

In that moment, Bella realized why he had brought her to the brothel first thing this morning. He hadn't wanted to test her, rather he'd wanted to warn her that this job would be hard, both physically and emotionally, and it would require a level of courage Bella wasn't sure she had.

Just then, Jesus's words to his disciples came to mind. *I tell you the truth, whatever you did for the least of these brothers of mine, you did for Me.*

This work was vastly important for the Kingdom. And Dr. Shane had asked her to share in it with him.

Her very soul trembled at the implication.

Singing opera might have brought a moment's enjoyment to others, perhaps even a brief respite in a complicated world, but this—this caring for the sick—was infinitely more significant than memorizing an aria or hitting a difficult note.

"Miss O'Toole, would you be so kind as to hand me the elixir in the clear bottle on your left?"

Determined to prove herself invaluable, she fixed her mind on the task at hand. "Of course."

Just as she made her way around the bed, the door swung open with a bang.

Bella spun around at the noise.

"What is the meaning of this outrage?" said an angry female voice from the shadows.

Dr. Shane blew out a frustrated breath and cast his gaze to the heavens. "Not now. Please, Lord, not now."

He quickly lowered his head and shot Bella a pained expression. "Brace yourself."

With another deep inhale, he swiveled toward the woman who now stood silhouetted in the dim lighting from the hallway.

"Miss Silks," he began with forced patience. "I am attending Lizzie at the moment. Please be so kind as to wait outside until I call for you."

In spite of the doctor's request, the woman swept boldly into the room. Each step she took was calculated, carefully placed and used for absolute effect. Bella should know. She'd trained for years to avoid making such an obvious entrance.

Dr. Shane muttered something under his breath, but Bella was too busy watching Mattie Silks to decipher his meaning.

With her gold satin dress, matching gloves and over-tight bodice, the woman was a complete caricature of herself. She might have been a great beauty once, but the icy glare, unnatural blond hair and overplucked eyebrows made her look hard now, almost manly.

Her sharp gaze arced through the room, halted a moment on the ill woman in the bed. Bella thought she saw a show of compassion in the depths of those inflexible blue eyes but the moment passed and Bella found herself on the receiving end of an unbending glare.

Well, Bella had spent too many years fighting her way to the top of her profession to let an amateur intimidate her with such transparent tactics.

Slanting her own challenging glance in the woman's direction, Bella drew herself to her full height and locked gazes with the surly madam.

Mattie bristled.

Bella smiled. Sweetly.

Wrathful sparks flew between them like sabers.

"Who are you?" Mattie demanded. Her voice came out gravelly, as though she had only just awakened from a fitful sleep or had yet to go to bed for the night.

Judging from the attire, Bella decided on the latter.

She also decided the rude question warranted no response from her.

"I asked you a question, girl."

Casting himself in the role of protector—the dear man—Dr. Shane released a low growl, moved around the bed and positioned his large body between Bella and the indignant madam.

"This is my new assistant," he said, gently shifting Bella farther behind him. "And I would ask you not to bother her as she is in the midst of performing duties for me."

He was playing his part to perfection, all the way down to the fierce scowl on his face. How…sweet.

And completely unnecessary.

Squaring her shoulders, Bella brushed around her gentle lion.

"I assure you, I am only here to assist Dr. Shane in his daily tasks, Miss Silks. Nothing more." Might as well make *that* perfectly clear.

Mattie ran her gaze all the way down to Bella's toes and back up, stopping at a few spots along the way on the return journey.

"That hideous attire does not fool me." Mattie waved a hand between them. "You are no nurse. And you look familiar. Did Emma Bradley send you?"

Bella cocked her head at the odd direction of their conversation. "Emma who?"

"Don't play ignorant." Mattie pointed a finger at Bella and shook it. "Emma Bradley is my fiercest competitor, as you well know."

Lizzie chose that moment to cough up a lung.

Bella made a face at the madam and quickly rushed

to attend her patient. As she'd done before, she moved in behind the sick woman and lifted her thin shoulders off the bed.

Concern written on his face, Dr. Shane touched Lizzie's forehead with his fingertips. "She's hot."

"Is that normal?" Bella asked.

He gave a slight, almost imperceptible shake of his head. But when he spoke he used the calm baritone she was beginning to think of as his "doctor" voice. "Don't worry, Lizzie. I have some medicine that will ease your suffering."

The moment he stepped back, Mattie Silks rushed forward. She grabbed his shoulder and forced him to turn until he was facing her again.

"I demand to know who this girl is." She narrowed her eyes at Bella like a woman plotting murder. "Tell me now, or I'll have Jack throw the both of you out on your ears."

Dr. Shane ignored the verbal threat and simply shook his head at the obnoxious woman. "Mattie, as usual, you're overreacting. Miss Bella is my assistant." His lips pulled into a mocking grin. "And since you asked so nicely, her full name is Isabella Constance…*O'Toole*."

"O'Toole?" Her eyes flicked over Bella in disbelief. "As in Beauregard O'Toole?"

"Correct. My assistant is the reverend's sister."

Mattie tapped a finger against her chin. "His sister, you say?"

Dr. Shane blessed her with a mild shrug, as though he had all the time in the world to prove his point.

Still tapping her chin, Mattie studied Bella through narrowed eyelids.

"Well, then. That's *new* information." She heaved a dramatic sigh and waved a dismissive gesture in Bella's general direction. "Carry on."

Without further comment, Mattie Silks spun on her heel and left the room.

Bella blinked at the spot the infamous madam had previously occupied. "What just happened?"

"Mattie Silks happened," came the doctor's droll response.

She turned her head to look at him. For a moment, they simply stared at one another in silent camaraderie.

"Is that right," she said at last.

"The woman is an event unto herself," he added with a sardonic grin spreading across his lips.

"That's one way of putting it," Bella muttered.

He chuckled. "Miss Silks will grow on you. In time."

"Grow on me?" Bella shuddered at the thought. "Might I remind you, doctor, that mold, pestilence and all kinds of hideous diseases *grow* on people."

His lips twitched, but he maintained his composure like the true gentleman he was. "At least the drama has passed for now."

Bella failed to agree with that inaccurate statement.

In her estimation, the drama had only just begun.

Chapter Eight

Sunday morning brought cold, icy rain and the perfect reason to sleep in. Unfortunately, Bella could not indulge in such luxury. Beau would expect her to attend church with the rest of the family. He'd probably insist she sit in the front pew with Hannah and Mavis. Which, of course, would bring speculation from the rest of the congregation.

Bella would have to explain her unexpected visit and new position as Dr. Shane's assistant. All with a pleasant smile on her face.

"Oh, Lord, please. Not yet." Her heart gave two hard knocks. "I'm not ready."

Flopping on her back, Bella clasped the locket around her neck with a tight fist and stared at the tiled ceiling. The rain continued its steady scratching against the window in an unbroken knot of gloom and doom.

All the while, one question kept gnawing at her. Why couldn't she fully repent of her mistake with William and allow God to heal her broken heart?

Sudden tears blurred her vision, making it impossible to decipher the patterns swirling above her.

Bella desperately wanted to become the good Christian woman she'd been before William had entered her life. But she didn't know how.

Bella yanked the covers over her head and sorted through the bigger dilemma confronting her this morning.

How could she walk into the Lord's House and face her Heavenly Father knowing sin still lived in her heart?

Familiar guilt came hard and fast. She rolled over and buried her head under the pillow. She'd nearly destroyed a marriage. Not that she'd known at the time. But she should have. All the signs had been there. William's elusive schedule, for one. Always available at night, never present during the day.

Because she'd wanted to believe in William's love for her, Bella had stubbornly refused to see the truth. And didn't that make her as guilty as her viscount? Yes, and thus she wore his necklace as a reminder.

Bella burrowed deeper under the covers and tried to think up a reason to skip church.

Perhaps she could pretend illness.

Sitting up, she tested out a cough, tried for a sniffle. No good.

Beau would know she was faking and call her bluff, perhaps even summon Dr. Shane. No. Out of the question. Pretending illness was not an option. Shane Bartlett could not think ill of her. Bella would not allow it.

She punched air into the feather pillow. "What to do. What to do."

Perhaps she could claim she had another engagement. But where?

And with whom?

It would have to be someone who wouldn't be attending church this morning. Someone who wouldn't ask too many questions. A woman with her own hidden secrets. Yes, of course. That was it.

With Lizzie's pale, thin face in mind, Bella tossed the covers off her legs and quickly dressed for the day. While she was lacing up her boots, a firm knock came at her door.

Beau.

On full alert, Bella set her chin at a stubborn angle and rose. "Come in."

Smiling, Beau stuck his head into the room. He smiled. Broadly. "Ah, good. You're up."

She spun in a circle. "And dressed, too."

His smile widened. One look at that boyish grin and Bella knew Hannah had told him the news of his impending fatherhood at last. For a moment, Bella simply stared at her brother with wistfulness. At the sight of all that joy, she felt strangely unmoored, disoriented.

Left out.

Now…really…when had she grown so selfish?

Disgusted with the direction of her own thoughts, Bella forced an answering smile across her lips. "You're certainly happy this morning." She knew her voice sounded too sharp, too bitter, so she struggled to lighten her tone. "May I ask the cause?"

He leaned a shoulder against the doorjamb, his gaze

filling with satisfaction. "God has blessed me more than I can fathom."

She waited for the rest.

"I'm going to be a father."

With those simple, heartfelt words, Bella's own concerns faded and she rushed to hug him. "Oh, Beau. I'm so pleased." And she was. Her brother deserved a happy family of his own. With a wife who adored him.

But now that Bella was sheltered in his arms, a deep sadness warred against her pleasure. With the conflicting emotions battling inside her, she clung a little longer than usual.

"You'll make a great father," she whispered, tears slipping along her lashes.

"Ah, Bella." He pulled back and wiped an errant tear away with his thumb. "I hate to see you so sad."

Good, solid Beau. He always worried about others first, never himself. Why did he have to be so good?

"I'm happy for you and Hannah," she said. "Truly. I am." But the loneliness was too loud in her voice, too thick and obvious for her words to ring true.

"Bella. Bella." Beau exhaled slowly. "I can't help you if you won't tell me what happened in London."

"I just needed a break," she said. "Nothing more."

"There's more." He dropped his gaze over her, shook his head. "But I know you well enough to know you won't reveal the full story until you're ready."

Relieved he wasn't going to force her to confide her secret, Bella hugged him once again. And tried not to sob into his shirt.

He patted her head like he had when she was little, and then set her at arm's length. "Church begins in less than an hour. Come eat and we'll be off."

Here it was. The moment of truth. "I...I won't be there." Her gaze chased around the room, landing everywhere but on Beau. "I have to see a patient this morning."

His gaze turned direct, making him look like a man who knew when people were lying to him. "Where are you seeing this patient?"

Dropping her gaze to the toe of her boot, Bella bit down on her lip. "Mattie's."

"You're going to a brothel?"

Bella jerked her chin at him. "Yes."

"Now?"

"No one visits prostitutes on Sunday mornings. It's time someone did, for all the right reasons."

She knew she sounded bitter. Well, she *felt* bitter. Memories of William's indecent proposal poked at her. Women like Lizzie—like Bella—like all of Mattie's girls—were good enough for an evening's entertainment, but never good enough for respectable marriage proposals.

"I see."

"No, you don't."

Beau sighed. Heavily. "Then explain it to me, Bella. Help me to understand why you would choose to spend Sunday morning at a brothel rather than in worship."

Bella lifted a careless shoulder. "Don't make this more complicated than it is. Lizzie needs me." She reached to her bedside table. "And look, I'm bringing my Bible."

Beau's eyes went dark and turbulent, reminding

Bella that her brother might be a compassionate preacher but he wasn't stupid. "A very realistic prop, little sister."

"How dare you."

"Am I wrong?"

It was her turn to sigh. Heavily. "Not completely. But Lizzie does need me."

"Fine, Bella. Have it your way." Annoyance spiked his voice to a lower octave than usual. "I won't force you to come to church."

"Thank you."

"And I suppose some good will come of this." Beau crossed his arms over his chest and held her gaze. "There's no better cure for despondency than caring for the sick."

Disappointment had Bella biting down on her lip. It was obvious Beau didn't understand her motives for avoiding church. How could he? He'd never veered from the godly path the Lord had set before him. Not once.

How could a man who always made the right decision ever understand Bella's shame? Her regret?

It would seem her ugly little secret must remain hidden inside her forever. Unfortunately, no peace came with the realization, no triumph. Just bone-weary loneliness. And a strong sense she was making another mistake. This one larger than the first, and far more life altering.

Heavy-hearted, and from a safe distance, Bella watched Lizzie struggle for every breath. With each labored intake, Bella found herself sucking air into her own lungs with the same sporadic rhythm. Before meeting this woman, she would never have believed anyone could live through such agony.

How could Shane Bartlett confront such misery, day in and day out, with no end in sight? Because he was strong and good and anointed by God to heal the sick.

Realizing how much she was growing to admire the man, Bella pressed a hand to her throat. Dr. Shane was drawing feelings out of her no one—not even William—had before.

Fear began unfurling in her heart. Oh, no. No, no. Bella would not fall for another man. Not now. Not like this. Not so soon. She had to be careful this time. She had to be smart, and in control.

The first step was to focus on the reason she'd come to Mattie's in the first place.

Poor, poor Lizzie.

The illness was clearly taking its toll. The woman looked exhausted, her faded green eyes hopeless, as though she'd long ago given up on ever leading a happy, normal life.

Had Lizzie left her dreams behind, or had her dreams failed her somewhere along the way?

Would Bella become this woman one day if she didn't take care?

After covering her face with a cloth like Dr. Shane had taught her, Bella wrung out a rag from the washbasin and scooted toward the edge of the bed. She placed the wet rag onto Lizzie's forehead.

"There," she said. "That should help relieve some of the heat."

Lizzie relaxed into her pillow and sighed. "Thank you, Miss O'Toole."

"Call me Bella."

A hint of a smile crossed the sick woman's lips. "Thank you, Bella."

Smiling, Bella picked up the woman's hand and gripped it between her own. Words of encouragement seemed trite, yet she didn't know Lizzie well enough to discuss anything of real importance.

Perhaps she should start small. "Does Lizzie stand for Elizabeth?" she asked.

"It does. I…" Lizzie struggled through a breath, and then another before continuing in a stilted tone. "I chose it after my favorite literary character, Elizabeth Bennett."

Pleasure swamped Bella at the declaration. The Jane Austen story was one of her favorites. Feeling a genuine connection now, she gave Lizzie's hand an affectionate squeeze and quoted the famous first line from *Pride and Prejudice*. "It is a truth universally acknowledged, that a single man in possession of a good fortune, must be in want of a wife."

Lizzie didn't actually grin in response, but her eyes crinkled at the edges.

"If I were to find a copy of the book, would you like me to read it to you?" Bella asked.

"I…" Lizzie's chin trembled. "Oh, yes. Please."

Heart hammering, Bella felt a rush of excitement. At last, she had found a way to offer comfort to this sad woman. "I will search out a copy this very afternoon."

Lizzie looked especially pleased, but then her gaze flicked to the doorway and her eyes widened.

Bella looked over her shoulder, caught sight of Mattie Silks standing in the doorway. "Good day, Miss Silks," she said without moving away from Lizzie.

The madam's eyebrows lifted at a proud angle. "Good day, Miss O'Toole."

Sighing, Bella rubbed a finger over her temple and wished she had a quick, pithy remark that would send the disturbing woman on her way.

Seconds ticked by before Mattie sailed into the room and lowered her gaze to Lizzie's face. The sorrow in the madam's eyes made her appear less harsh, accessible even. There could be no doubt she cared for this woman.

"I have a copy of *Pride and Prejudice* in my parlor," she said as she continued to stare at Lizzie's limp form.

Despite the hostility they'd shared at their first meeting, Bella wasn't prepared to alienate the madam completely. Not for Lizzie's sake, at any rate. "Would it be a bother if I asked to borrow the book, Miss Silks?"

Shifting away from the bed, Mattie regarded her with a long, serious expression. She remained silent so long, Bella feared the woman would refuse her request but then she said, "Come with me."

Bella shared a quick look with Lizzie when Mattie turned on her heels and left the room without a second glance.

"I'll be right back," Bella called over her shoulder.

Trotting to catch up, she uncovered her face and fell into step with the madam. A cold draft swept through the hallway, bringing the oddly pleasant scent of jasmine and musk. She hadn't expected that. Bella shivered in spite of herself and crossed her arms around her middle.

Mattie chose that moment to break the silence. "I would have expected a preacher's sister to be in church on a Sunday morning."

Bella ignored the feminine triumph in the madam's eyes and pretended grave interest in the crown molding running along the ceiling of the hallway. "I wanted to visit some of my new patients at a more leisurely pace. Sunday morning can be a lonely time if one cannot leave the bed."

"And yet the doctor feels the need to go to church."

Bella made a noncommittal sound. Why start an argument when they were getting on so well?

To her credit, the madam continued the rest of their trek without speaking again. In blessed silence, she led Bella down a back stairwell, past the kitchen and inside a small parlor.

As expected, the decor was as gaudy as the rest of the brothel. Yet there was a sense of homeyness here that transcended the tacky red and gold furnishings, as though this room was meant for the madam's private use only.

Best of all, shelves lined an entire wall and were filled with books from top to bottom.

Who would have thought Mattie Silks was a reader?

She eyed Bella with a speculative glance. "Are you an actress or a singer or both?"

Bella took immediate offense at the blunt question. "You aren't much for small talk, are you, Miss Silks?"

With unexpected grace, Mattie lowered herself into a wingback chair and crossed her legs at the knees. "You carry yourself with great confidence, Miss O'Toole, especially for one so young. You must have trained all your life."

Surprised by the compliment, Bella found herself unable to do more than stare at the woman as she tried to understand the odd change in Mattie's behavior. She was different here, in this room, almost pleasant.

"I am an opera singer," Bella said in answer.

"Are you any good?" Mattie asked, swinging her foot to some unheard beat.

No one had ever asked Bella that question outright. Oddly enough, she found Mattie's interrogation refreshing, and thus decided to answer with complete honesty.

"The Lord has blessed me with a gift, Miss Silks. One I do not take lightly. Already I am winning lead roles from singers twice my age. If I continue to train and no damage comes to my voice, I will become the premiere opera singer of our day."

Mattie nodded. "Then you must continue to train."

"It's not that simple."

"Why not?"

How could Bella explain to this woman that if she continued to perform in the world she'd just escaped, she might well become some man's mistress?

Her experience with William had opened her eyes to the only type of man she would attract. If she didn't leave the stage, she might sacrifice her soul, her very salvation, for her dreams. When the singing was over she would be just another Lizzie, only in a more comfortable cage.

And yet, singing opera was all she knew.

"I believe God has a different plan for me now."

Oh, Lord, please let that be true. Please, please, please.

Mattie looked at her oddly but didn't respond. Just as the silence grew uncomfortable, the madam shook her head sadly and rose from her chair.

With a flowing gait, she ambled over to the shelves, pulled out a book and handed the thin volume to Bella.

Bella slowly opened the cover. From the worn binding and curled pages she could see the novel had been read often.

"It's my favorite, too." Mattie touched Bella's hand. "I find great comfort in the happy ending."

Bella locked gazes with the older woman and a startling sense of understanding passed between them. The connection should have been disturbing, should have been terrifying, but it wasn't.

Had Bella found a kindred spirit in the notorious madam?

Perhaps underneath their individual professions, underneath their different life choices, Mattie Silks and Bella O'Toole were more alike than any would believe.

But did that make them objects of pity or women destined to become friends?

Chapter Nine

Just as Beau had suggested, Shane found his errant assistant hiding out in Lizzie's bedroom. He tried not to be disappointed, but he couldn't ignore the fact that Miss O'Toole had chosen to spend Sunday morning in a brothel instead of church.

Leaning against the doorjamb, he studied the mysterious woman who seemed to surprise him at every turn. She certainly made a pretty picture, perched gracefully on a chair next to the bed. Her head was bent over a book. And as she read aloud, her soft, lilting accent imparted a whimsical mood in the otherwise austere room.

Shifting his focus to Lizzie, Shane marveled at the change in his patient. With her eyes half-closed, she looked the most peaceful he'd seen her in weeks.

Out of the corner of his eye, he caught a flutter of material and realized there was a third occupant. Mattie Silks sat in a chair on the other side of the bed, holding herself serenely, pleasantly. Quietly!

Shane blinked.

At the sight of the three most unlikely women sitting together, an eerie sense of déjà vu whipped through him. In their own way, each reminded him of his mother.

Lizzie was the woman his mother had become in her final months. Worn out, sick, beyond all reasonable hope.

Mattie was the woman his mother might have become had she lived. A woman who had outlasted the mistakes of her youth and now did what she thought she had to do to survive the harsh world around her.

Lastly, there was Miss O'Toole. Despite the seemingly innocent picture she presented to the world, she reminded him of the mother from his youth. Beautiful, full of promise, the personification of possibilities. And just like his mother, Shane sensed Miss O'Toole was one bad choice away from a dark, dismal future.

Which was absurd, and probably a case of bad lighting. Bella O'Toole was the daughter of solid Christian parents and the sister of a dedicated preacher. She was nothing like Amanda Bartlett.

Yet…what did Shane really know about the woman he'd hired to assist him?

Was she ministering to Lizzie out of charity, as it would seem on the surface? Or had some other motive brought her here today, something less respectable? Something unthinkable.

A muscle locked in his jaw.

Pushing from the doorway, he cleared his throat and stepped into the room.

Miss O'Toole lifted her gaze from the page. At the

same moment, a rogue sunbeam kissed the top of her head, casting a thousand shades of gold in its wake.

Shane froze. All thought evaporated into a black void.

Seemingly caught in the same trance, Miss O'Toole held his glance. After a moment, however, her gaze softened, warmed. And his pulse scrambled.

How could a simple look hold such power?

Slowly, distant sounds broke through his mind, piece by piece: the rocking of a chair, the ticking of a clock, his own shattered breathing.

And *still* he stared.

Blushing, Miss O'Toole lowered her gaze. She stumbled over a sentence, sighed and then closed the book. "Dr. Shane, we weren't expecting to see you this afternoon."

When her gaze met his again he found the connection between his brain and his mouth had disappeared.

With a rustle of skirts, Mattie sprang to her feet, drawing his attention away from Miss O'Toole at last.

"What a pleasant surprise...doctor." Her tone said otherwise.

"Mattie," he replied on an equally flat note. From the calculating gleam in her eyes, Shane knew better than to engage the madam in further conversation.

Of course, what he did—or did not do—hardly mattered. This was Mattie Silks. Nothing on his part could deter her once she'd resolved to have a bit of fun at his expense.

Swishing her hips in a telling manner, she made her way across the room straight to him. "Dare I hope this is a social call?" she asked. "Have you admitted to your loneliness at long last?"

Shane frowned. Mattie had asked him that question often enough. He usually had a witty comeback that shut her up. But he would not play her game today, especially in front of the other women. "I am here to see to my patient, Miss Silks. As always."

She seemed to accept his response, but then he made a fundamental mistake. He glanced at Miss O'Toole.

Mattie, of course, followed his gaze.

Eyes narrowed, she measured. Calculated. Then flipped him a knowing smile. "So it's like that, is it?"

Swallowing back a hasty response, Shane forced a bland expression on his face.

"I came to fetch Miss O'Toole, as well." His tone came out lower and deadlier than he had planned. "Her brother is worried about her."

Smirking, Mattie placed a well-manicured hand on his arm and relaxed into a hip-thrusting pose. "Now, doctor, why the pretense? We both know *you* were the one worried about our lovely opera singer."

He glared at the talons wrapped around his arm. When she didn't release him right away, he moved out of reach. "Don't be obvious, Mattie. It does you no credit."

"Me?" She laughed. A short, tinkling, terrible sound of glee. "Maybe you should glance at your face in the mirror over there," she pointed her thumb over her right shoulder, "and see what 'obvious' really looks like."

Shane pressed his lips into a flat line. "I'm warning you. Don't start. Not today."

"And I'm warning you." Mattie's eyes hardened. "Remember who you're dealing with, *doctor.*"

Shane opened his mouth to end the childish battle but was interrupted by Miss O'Toole's soft sigh. "Dr. Shane. Please…" Her voice flowed into another sigh.

Shane switched his full attention to her and waited for the rest.

"I…that is…" She quickly cast her eyes to the book in her lap, chipped at the binding with her fingernail. "Please be so kind as to tell my brother there is no need to worry. As you can see, I am quite well."

Shane saw no such thing.

Not only was Miss O'Toole keeping company with a notorious madam, he'd caught the quick slice of shame in her eyes before she'd lowered her gaze. The gesture reminded him that Bella O'Toole was more than his friend's innocent sister, more than his competent assistant. She was a woman harboring a secret, one she refused to reveal to her brother or anyone else.

An ugly thought occurred to him. Had Miss O'Toole shared her worries with Mattie Silks or even Lizzie?

Frustration reared, and something darker, uglier, but he fought back the troubling emotions. What did it matter who Miss O'Toole shared her secret with? He had enough to worry about without adding a beautiful, wounded opera singer to the long list of people who needed him.

But, in this, Shane knew he lied to himself. He *wanted* this woman to turn to him. He wanted to be her confidant, her *only* confidant. The strength of the wish nearly knocked him to his knees. He felt the shock in his gut. *In his heart.*

Needing to return to familiar ground, he cleared his mind of all thought save one. "I'd like to examine Lizzie now."

Miss O'Toole rose. "Of course. Miss Silks was on her way out when you arrived." She shot Mattie a pleading look. "Weren't you?"

The madam stared at her for several seconds. A silent message passed between them and then, wonder of wonders, Mattie slowly nodded. "Of course. I'll leave you to your business."

Without looking at Lizzie or Shane, Mattie retrieved the book from Miss O'Toole and headed for the door. Stopping at the threshold, she looked back over her shoulder. "Bella?"

"Yes?"

"You may borrow this anytime you wish." She waved the book above her head. "You know where to find it."

"I certainly do. And thank you. It's a very kind offer." A genuine smile spread across Miss O'Toole's lips. "One I plan to accept often."

Mattie appeared ready to say more but she snapped her head around and left the room without another word.

At this odd interaction between the unlikcly pair, a jolt of alarm spread through Shane. Mattie might have a soft spot deep, deep, deep, *deep* in her heart, but she was also a shrewd businesswoman, ruthless to the point of cruelty when she wanted something. Or someone.

Was she befriending Miss O'Toole for her own end?

Shane didn't have time to contemplate that awful thought before the door clicked shut, and Miss O'Toole turned into his assistant once again.

"You'll be glad to know Lizzie's feeling much better today." She removed the compress from their patient's forehead and dipped it in the bowl next to the bed. "Aren't you, dear?"

Lizzie smiled up at her. "Much."

Recognizing Miss O'Toole's closed expression, Shane held on to his questions—for now—and moved deeper into the room. With a flick of his wrist, he shed his coat. After rolling up his sleeves, he took Lizzie's wrist in one hand and pulled out his watch with the other.

All business now, he counted the heartbeats, pleased to discover her pulse thumped strongly against his fingertips. Her coloring was good today, less ashy, and her face wasn't as drawn as usual. For a brief moment, he allowed himself to believe she might recover. At least long enough to change the condition of her soul, if not her body.

Healing the sick was what Shane had been called to do, especially women with nowhere else to turn for medical care. But their salvation mattered more. If he could afford them enough time to resolve their relationship with God then he'd fulfilled one of his purposes in life.

Unfortunately, he'd never known his mother's heart, or whether she'd turned to Jesus in her final moments of life. He'd been too young and too caught up in his bitterness toward his father to care enough to pursue the matter. He hadn't even prayed for her soul. For that alone, he'd failed her.

He would not fail the others.

With that thought, he caught Miss O'Toole's eye.

She was staring at him, her gaze full of concern, as though she could read his troubled thoughts.

A reflex to share the pain of his distress came fast. His eyes stung from the effort to form his thoughts into words. Just as he started to speak, he was hit by a wall of common sense and kept his mouth shut.

He had to remember Miss O'Toole's presence in his life was temporary. All too soon she would leave for London or New York or some other world stage miles away from Colorado.

Unlike his mother, Shane would not fall for someone out of reach. He ignored the small whisper in his head that suggested it might be too late.

"Dr. Bartlett, you left your coat," Bella called after his retreating back.

He turned to look at her with an absent expression on his face. "What coat?"

She waved the garment in her hand. "This one."

"Ah." He gave her a sheepish grin. "That one."

With clipped steps, he returned to her side.

As she helped him shrug into his coat, a wave of fondness crashed over her and she had to resist the urge to smooth the dark fabric across his broad shoulders. Balling her hands into fists, she followed him out of Lizzie's room and down the long hallway that led to the front stairwell.

Walking silently next to the doctor, Bella realized she

had learned a few truths about the man in their week-long acquaintance. Although brilliant, he spoke to his patients in a way that made them feel accepted, and heard. He was truly a compassionate healer who also carried the burden of his patients' pain in his heart, even if he refused to acknowledge that fact out loud.

In spite of the distance he kept between him and the rest of the world, she saw his goodness, his integrity.

And the more time she spent around Shane Bartlett, the more she wondered what it would be like to share the healthy give and take of a relationship with a godly man. She was sure it would be nothing like her involvement with William.

Lord Crawley had offered her protection and worldly luxury. But he'd never offered himself. Or his life.

How had Bella missed that?

Easy enough. She'd been dazzled by William's dark masculine beauty, by his well-timed compliments, and by her own love for him.

But, truly, how could she have loved such a man? When wonderful, decent men like Shane Bartlett existed in the world. She cast him a quick glance, then sighed at the truth that flashed through her mind.

She wasn't good enough for men like Shane.

She'd accepted William's suit because deep down she'd sensed the awful truth about herself. She had deserved nothing better than what William had offered.

Swallowing back a rising sob, she followed the doctor down the steep stairwell. Perhaps her lack of goodness explained her affinity for Mattie Silks and

Lizzie. In their company she felt less sinful by comparison. Oh, she knew she was deluding herself. There was no hierarchy of sin in the Lord's eyes. All sin was wrong and led to separation from God. But knowing a thing and believing it were two separate matters.

Drawing close to the main floor, she looked around her, desperate to rid herself of her depressing thoughts. Unfortunately, the gaudiness and sour smells matched the ugliness of her soul. Would she ever be cleansed of her sins? Was she destined to live a life as black as her soul, like the women who conducted their business here?

Her eyes filled with tears and she nearly collided into Dr. Shane as he drew to a sudden stop.

"Oh." She stepped away too quickly and fell backward, landing on the bottom step.

"Miss O'Toole." The concern in the doctor's voice made her feel…worse.

He offered her his hand. "My apologies."

For a tense moment she stared at his outstretched fingers. This competent, compassionate man was simply offering her his assistance, nothing more. Why, then, did she sense he was asking her a question? And that her answer mattered.

No, she was being overly dramatic. An unpleasant character trait she was only just discovering about herself.

Gathering her courage, she placed her hand in his, palm to palm. As his fingers closed over hers, a sense of calm rippled through her.

Staring into her eyes, he pulled her to her feet, blinked and then quickly released her hand. His gaze, however, stayed locked firmly with hers, as it had in Lizzie's room. And just like earlier, all that intensity directed at Bella made her feel wrapped in safety.

It was an uncomfortable, thoroughly wonderful sensation.

"Are you all right?" He shoved at his hair, leaving a few ends sticking out when he pulled his hand away. "You appear upset."

If only he knew the half of it. "I am quite well," she said with enough over-the-top enthusiasm to make her sound like a rank amateur.

Disgusted with her inability to tap into her usual poise around this man, she took a step back, forced her gaze to a spot on the tip of her shoes. "I always find it hard to leave Lizzie."

He placed a finger under her chin and applied gentle pressure until she looked at him again.

"Why is that?" he asked, his voice soothing. He was in full doctor mode, but there was something more personal in his eyes. For the first time since leaving London, Bella wanted to confess all. To him. *Only him.*

Would he understand? Or would he pity her? Once he knew her secret, would he shove her into a different category of women and quit looking at her as if she mattered, truly mattered?

Bella couldn't bear the possibility of this man thinking less of her. That, she realized, would be far worse than what William had done to her.

"Miss O'Toole," he urged. "Tell me why you find it hard to leave Lizzie."

She took note of his patient expression and was suddenly frightened. And oddly hopeful. Confused. And so very, very sad. "I…I don't want her to be alone."

Which was true enough.

"She has a house full of women around her."

Which was also true. And completely beside the point. "It's not the same. They don't understand her."

"And you do?"

Pressing her hands palm to palm, she threaded her fingers tightly together. "Yes."

He reached out, laid a hand on her shoulder. "Are you trying to save her soul?"

He was so handsome, so pure-minded that she answered with complete honesty. "No. I am far from qualified."

"No one is qualified," he said gently. "As your own brother has said often enough, we humans plant the seeds. God does the rest."

At the utter conviction in his voice, Bella clasped the necklace around her throat and whispered, "Perhaps I have no seed to plant."

He stared at her so long that Bella was sure he could see straight into her soul. "Give it time."

Bella sighed. "Yes, of course."

But she feared time was running out for her. If she didn't atone for her sin soon she might never be able to come back into the fold. And where would that leave her then?

Chapter Ten

Several mornings later, Bella stood alone in Beau and Hannah's kitchen. Having slept poorly, her steps were sluggish as she headed to the window overlooking the backyard.

A misty fog slithered along the frozen ground, twisting around the base of each tree. A patch of pearly gray light hit the branches above declaring that a new day dawned. But Bella found no joy in the promise of a fresh morning.

Cold air slipped its icy fingers through a seam between glass and casement. Bella shivered. Familiar tension knotted along her spine. Seeking relief, she closed her eyes and clasped her hands together. *Dear Heavenly Father—*

She cut herself off, desperately searching for the right words to pray. None came. She could confess her sin for the thousandth time, but it wouldn't take away what she'd done. Oh, she knew her God was a forgiving God. She just couldn't seem to forgive herself.

What had Paul said to the Ephesians? Something about forgetting what was behind and straining toward what was ahead. Yet, how could Bella move forward when she couldn't let go of the past?

Opening her eyes, she wrapped her fingers around William's locket and tugged. Hard. As always, she released the necklace before the chain broke.

Hot tears of frustration stung her eyes. What was wrong with her? Why couldn't she remove the wretched piece of jewelry?

Oh, Lord, help me. Guide me.

"Bella?" Hannah's soft voice sliced through her thoughts. "May I join you?"

Bella spun around to face her sister-in-law. "Of... of course."

Hannah glided farther into the room. Thankfully, instead of dragging Bella into a conversation, she held out her hand and produced a sealed letter. "This came for you yesterday." She rolled it in her palm. "It looks important."

At the sight of the expensive paper, Bella sucked in a tight breath. One glance was all it took for her to recognize William's seal. Her entire body turned ice-cold. She needed to sit, but she gathered her courage and accepted the letter with trembling fingers before her legs collapsed and she dropped into a nearby chair.

She'd half dreaded, half hoped this day would come, the day William recognized his mistake and called her back to him. But now that he had found her, Bella felt nothing. Wanted nothing. *Believed* nothing.

Nothing. Nothing. Nothing.

With little worry lines forming between her eyebrows, Hannah stooped in front of her and rested her hand on Bella's knee. "I see I was right not to show this to your brother."

Bella nodded, gulped in a ragged breath.

"It's from a man." Hannah said the words as a statement.

Unable to answer, Bella could only stare at her sister-in-law. She needed more control, less confusion. But her mind refused to cooperate.

"Is he the reason you left London?"

Biting her bottom lip, Bella studied the red seal with the viscount's family crest pressed into the wax. "I… I…I don't know how he found me."

"He?"

The muscles in her stomach quivered. "William Gordon, Lord Crawley."

"A suitor?"

"Yes." Bella rubbed a shaky palm along the top of her thigh, shuttered. "No. Not in the way you would think."

Tugging one of Bella's hands into hers, Hannah spoke very softly. "Bella, whatever has happened, whatever he did to you, you can tell me."

Bella fought back tears, a useless indulgence when control was needed. She wanted to rail, to pound her fists in the air. She sighed instead. "You wouldn't understand."

"You might be surprised." Hannah kept her voice low. "For years I traveled with an acting troupe. Your brother, Tyler, was one of the more notorious members.

Thanks to his example alone, I've seen my share of shocking behavior." She gave Bella an ironic smile. "He did run off with my sister, after all. My *engaged* sister."

Of course. Bella knew the ugly details well enough. The scandal was still a sore subject in her family. Tyler had been wrong to travel alone with Hannah's sister without the benefit of marriage, especially when she was engaged to another man. Tyler meant well, most of the time, but he could be selfish and an unconscionable rogue of the first order. Hannah had seen him at his worst.

Hot shame spread through Bella, shame for what Tyler had done to this woman and her family. No, Bella would not allow Beau's new wife to discover that yet another member of the famous O'Toole family had a sinful heart.

"I'm sorry, Hannah." She drew her hand free. "I…can't."

A look of disappointment spread across the other woman's face. "I won't press. But when you're ready, I'll be here to listen. No judgment. No condemnation."

Shaken by her sister-in-law's kindness, Bella refused to do anything so dramatic as cry.

"I'll leave you to your letter now." Hannah gave her hand one last pat, rose and then left the kitchen with her typical grace.

Alone again, Bella turned the letter over and over in her hand. The monumental significance of William actually finding her here in Colorado was staggering. Frightening.

What could he possibly have to say to her now? Had

his circumstances changed? Was he renewing his suit, this time with a more respectable end?

She fingered the locket around her neck. It felt lighter this morning. Surely, a trick of her imagination. After all, nothing had changed. Not for her.

Or had it? An image of Shane Bartlett flitted across her mind. Integrity. Courage. The doctor had both. Lord Crawley had little of either.

If Bella had an ounce of sense, she would toss William's letter in the nearest fire and that would be the end of that.

Unfortunately, Bella was discovering her ratio of sense to senselessness was far out of balance, with senselessness winning hands down.

Read it? Toss it?

She would decide later.

Shoving the paper into the pocket of her apron, she tried to put the matter out of her mind and focus on the day ahead.

Then again…

Perhaps she should read the letter now, just get it over with. Or perhaps she would look at it tonight, when she was alone, with endless hours of solitude stretching before her. Yes, maybe then, when there was no chance of interruption, she would read the words William had sent halfway across the world to her.

Or…maybe not.

Something had happened since Shane had last seen Miss O'Toole, something that put her on edge. She was pleasant enough, on the surface, but the difference was there. In her eyes. If he didn't know better he'd say she had the look his mother always had right before his father made his weekly visit—an odd mixture of hope and dread, melancholy and joy.

With his own emotions still in a tangle from Sunday afternoon, Shane chose to ignore the change in Miss O'Toole. Jaw tight, he stepped aside in order to allow her to enter Charity House ahead of him.

As usual, they were met at the door by Laney Dupree, Marc's wife and co-owner of the orphanage. Her arms were filled with a squirming miniature version of herself.

"Good morning, Laney." Shane reached out and ruffled her young daughter's hair. "Laurette. You're both looking fine this morning."

Laurette pulled her thumb out of her mouth and grinned. But Laney's face scrunched into a frown. "Shane. Miss O'Toole, thank God you've finally arrived."

She lowered her daughter to the ground. Laurette clutched Laney's skirt with one hand and held a doll tight against her chest with the other. Sensing her mother's tense mood, the child adopted an identical expression of worry on her face.

"What is it?" Miss O'Toole asked before Shane had a chance. "What's happened?"

"I don't know, precisely," Laney admitted, her gaze darting between them. "Six of the children came to me yesterday with runny noses and complaining of headaches, nothing we haven't seen before. I kept the lot of them home this morning and sent the rest on to school as usual. But in the last hour, two have grown worse."

By the end of her explanation, Shane was already striding for the stairs. "Did you separate the children from the rest?"

"Last night. I put the boys in the tiger room. The girls are in the castle room." She turned to Miss O'Toole, her eyes serious and worried, her hands wringing together in front of her. "We always try to keep the sick children separate from the rest. Illness can spread quickly."

A thick blanket of tension fell between them, but Miss O'Toole patted Laney's shoulder in a feminine gesture of solidarity. "Makes perfect sense to me."

Shane continued forward, stopped.

"What about the babies?" he asked.

"Megan is with them. She's kept them away from the others since yesterday."

Shane was glad to hear it. And especially grateful they only had two babies in residence at the moment. If illness spread they would be hit the hardest.

Conflicting emotions tugged at him but he shoved them out of his mind. He needed to gather as much information as possible and he needed to do it with a clear head. "Tell me the precise symptoms of each."

"All six have runny nose, coughing, sneezing and sore throats." Laney's tone never varied, her eyes never left his face, but Shane could feel her concern as though she were screaming at him. "Miles and Stacy have progressed to a loss of appetite."

On the surface, the symptoms could mean anything.

Various diagnoses were shooting around one another in his mind like moths to light.

A tug on his pant leg broke his concentration and he glanced down.

"Stacy has goo in her eyes," Laurette added gravely. "White goo."

That certainly narrowed down the possibilities. He looked up at Laney again. "Do they feel hot to the touch?"

Laney nodded.

All right then. The symptoms could mean bad colds. But Shane noted that neither Laney nor Laurette showed any signs of illness. Added to the "white goo" description he feared they had another case of measles on their hands. The disease had spread through the orphanage six months ago. Laney, Laurette and half of the children had suffered.

The other half had been spared, Miles and Stacy among them.

Shane turned to Miss O'Toole and asked her a question he should have asked long before now. "What childhood illnesses have you had?"

Urgency made his voice clipped. She didn't seem to mind. "Pox, mumps and measles."

"Good. Then let's go have a look."

One by one they started up the stairs, but Miss O'Toole held up her hand to stop Laney and Laurette. "You two stay here. At least until we know what we're dealing with."

Laney looked prepared to argue, but Miss O'Toole spoke again. "We don't want you and your daughter exposed."

Normally, Shane would have had Laney join him in the sickroom. However, that was before he'd hired an assistant, a very smart assistant who had recognized the larger ramifications before Shane had himself.

"Miss O'Toole is right," he said. "It would be better if you stayed downstairs. For now."

Laney shook her head, started forward.

Miss O'Toole laid a gentle hand on her arm. "I'll bring you a report as soon as we have more information."

Eyebrows slamming together, Laney tried to push forward but Laurette tugged on her hand. "Mama? Why are you so ang-ery?"

An odd sound came out of Laney's mouth, not quite a snort of frustration, not quite a sob.

Laurette popped her thumb in her mouth and whimpered.

With visible effort, Laney cleared her face of all emotion and forced a smile across her lips. "I'm not angry, baby. Just worried."

Laurette gave her a dubious look that had four-year-old doubt written all over it.

Laney closed her eyes and blew out a long sigh. "Why don't you come along and help me make bread for tonight's supper?"

"Really?" The child grinned around her thumb. "You never letted me do that before."

"There's always a first time." Laney lifted the child in her arms and hugged her tightly against her.

Laurette struggled. "You holding too tight."

Sighing, Laney shifted the child in her arms and

glanced at Miss O'Toole. "We'll be in the kitchen when you have more to tell me."

Before setting off in the opposite direction, Laney blessed Shane with a sharp glare of warning, as if to say he better remember she was waiting for news.

Shane barely noticed. He was too busy marveling at how Miss O'Toole had taken control of the situation.

Yet again, the woman had surprised him. He was starting to like the sensation. He was starting to like it a lot.

But then she quirked her eyebrow at him. "Let's get to work, shall we?"

Realizing he was staring and feeling like a besotted idiot, he turned slightly to his left and waved her forward. "After you."

She sent him a quick lovely smile as she passed, but her eyes remained distant. Just as well. There were six miserable children needing his complete attention.

He stared up at the ceiling. Once he focused on his patients, he would be immune to Miss O'Toole's surprises.

He was sure of it.

Of course, as self-deception went, this was one of his best efforts yet.

Chapter Eleven

From the bleak look on Dr. Shane's face, Bella expected a dismal prognosis. Nevertheless, she kept her opinions to herself as she joined him on the examination of each patient. Looking around, she realized she'd never been in this room before.

There were eight beds in all, with an equal number of matching chests of drawers. No expense had been spared. The high-quality design of the furniture spoke of an attention to detail that most orphanages ignored.

Of course, the exquisite furnishings were nothing compared to the murals on the walls. Bella now understood why Laney had referred to this as the castle room. The paintings brought to mind childhood fairy tales and happily-ever-afters. Each scene made Bella want to return to her innocent youth, where dreams still existed, where every boy would grow up to become a courageous knight and every girl a beautiful princess.

Along the top edges of the walls Bible verses had

been painted in a glorious, flowing script. She read one from Matthew 19, *Let the children come to me, and do not hinder them.* And another from Isaiah 43, *Fear not, for I have redeemed you. I have summoned you by name.* And her favorite, from Hebrews 13:5, *Never will I leave you; never will I forsake you.*

As she read the Scriptures silently to herself, Bella experienced an overwhelming sense of peace. It was as if God was wrapping His unconditional love around her and cloaking her in His warmth.

Dr. Shane's quick intake of breath had Bella turning her attention to him. He leaned over Kimberly, a girl of thirteen who was normally full of energy and good cheer. This morning, her cheeks looked flushed as she wrestled inside a fitful sleep.

"What can I do to help?" Bella whispered.

"Come closer." His words came out even, but Bella could tell by the slight tensing of his jaw and flare of his nostrils that he was deeply worried.

Bending over for a better look, Bella detected the beginnings of a blotchy rash on Kimberly's face. Stifling a gasp, she glanced at Dr. Shane. By the stress lines around his mouth, it was obvious he didn't like what he saw.

Bella didn't either.

Grim-faced, he nudged the girl awake with a gentle hand to her shoulder.

Kimberly moaned and her lashes fluttered open.

"Hi, there," he said in a serious tone. "I hear you're not feeling well."

"My head hurts. I ache everywhere." She kicked her legs out from under the covers. "And I'm hot. Really hot."

Don't forget cranky, Bella silently added.

Seemingly immune to the teenager's sour mood, Dr. Shane turned her head to the right and brushed a clump of hair behind her ear. "Miss O'Toole. Tell me what you see."

Bella studied the area he indicated. "The skin is red, looks like the rash is spreading."

"It is." He pointed to their patient's neck next. "But it hasn't spread there. Yet."

Dr. Shane turned Kimberly's head back toward him. "How long have you been feeling bad?"

"A couple days." Her eyes filled with tears. "What's wrong with me? Am I going to die?" she whimpered with dramatic emphasis.

An actress in the making. Bella liked her more and more.

Clearly amused by the performance, Dr. Shane smiled. "No, you're not going to die. But I need to check the other girls and boys before I make my final diagnosis."

His hands were so beautiful, Bella thought as she watched him sweep Kimberly's hair back over her ear, so full of healing. Bella wanted to weep, but she didn't understand why.

Surprised by her reaction, she caught her trembling bottom lip between her teeth and followed Dr. Shane to another young girl on the other side of the room.

This one looked decidedly worse. The rash had

moved to her neck and she had the infamous "white goo" in her eyes.

After checking behind her ears and studying the eye infection, Dr. Shane sighed. "It's what I feared."

Bella lifted her eyebrows.

"Measles."

The air in her lungs pulsated hot, then cold. "That's highly contagious, isn't it?"

Nodding, he raked both hands through his hair. "The only remedy is bed rest."

"I remember. A bad case whipped through our theater company when I was seven. I was confined to bed for a week." She eyed him carefully. "I'm surprised this hasn't hit the orphanage before now."

"It has. Six months ago. I'll have to retrieve my records to clarify which children contracted the disease last time." He scrutinized the room, his gaze sharp and measuring. "There may be more sick children before the day is out. The symptoms don't usually develop until about a week after a child has been exposed."

A week? "Oh."

He considered Bella with the same measuring look he'd shot around the room. "I'd like you to stay until the contagious period passes. In the meantime, I'll attend our other patients alone."

The panic started at her knees, moved up her spine and ended in a tremble that rattled the tips of her hair. "I…" Bella broke eye contact.

What could she say? That she didn't feel comfortable around the children? That she'd rather spend her time at Mattie's brothel where she couldn't do much damage to souls already tainted?

What would he think of her then?

What did that say about the selfish state of her heart?

Heavenly Father, give me the courage to put these little ones first, and please, please, keep my penchant for making bad decisions from rubbing off on them.

Misunderstanding her anxiety, Dr. Shane touched her hand. "There will be many moments of boredom, I'm sure. Is there anything I can do for you while I'm out? Anything I can bring from your brother's home?"

A little courage? "Nothing. No, wait. There is one thing you can do for me. I…"

"Yes?" he urged when she didn't continue.

Oddly nervous, Bella shifted from one foot to the other. "Will you check on Lizzie, let her know I won't be able to read to her for a while?"

He smiled with his eyes. "Consider it done."

The moment he turned to leave, Bella lowered her gaze back to Stacy. Without looking up, she called after him just as he crossed the threshold. "You forgot your coat."

"How did you know that? You're not even looking at me." His voice sounded both surprised and oddly frustrated, as though he wasn't sure he liked her knowing him so well.

Moving across the room, she lifted a shoulder. "I know because you always forget your coat."

She reached for the garment and held it out of reach when he tried to snatch it away from her. "Allow me."

He glared at her but then slowly stuck out one of his

arms. As was becoming their custom, she helped him shrug into the first sleeve and then the next.

When he turned back to face her, she tugged on the lapels and had to fight the urge to reach up and even out his hair where he'd pulled his fingers through the glossy chaos a few too many times.

In truth, the man was a mess. His future wife would have her hands full organizing him on a daily basis. She would have to be patient and kind, smart and fast on her feet. And, most of all, she would have to be willing to share him with his patients.

Did Bella want to be that fortunate woman? Was such a beautiful reality possible?

No. Wishful thinking, at best. After all, the sealed letter in her pocket reminded Bella of her real worth in a man's eyes.

Bella felt the urge to weep again. But this time, she knew exactly why.

After explaining the situation to Laney, Shane's next stop was his office. On his way, he passed the Charity House School, wondering how many children were already sick but weren't showing symptoms.

There wasn't much he could do at this point. His best defense was to gather his records as quickly as possible and return in time to examine the children who had missed the first round of measles.

For now, they were best left at school, away from the sicker ones.

Needing a moment to gather his thoughts, he drew

his horse to a stop and studied the school's building. The outside looked like the rest of the mansions in the neighborhood: sturdy, elegant and fashionable.

In seven short years, with diligence and a lot of prayer, Marc and Laney Dupree had created a safe haven within a larger, harsher world of prejudice and hatred. It had begun with Charity House, had expanded to the addition of the school, and now, thanks to Beauregard O'Toole and his gifted wife, there was a church.

God's hand was clearly at work.

And Shane wanted to do his part for the effort. His dream was to add a clinic nearby, perhaps even a connecting shelter for women in trouble. But that would take money. And since most of his patients didn't have the funds to pay for his services, he was far short of an acceptable down payment. God willing, the funding would come one day and then Shane's clinic would become a reality.

Refusing to lose faith, no matter the odds stacked against him, Shane flicked his horse's reins and steered his wagon toward town.

The Rocky Mountains stood on his left, God's handiwork evident in their stark beauty. The cool air felt clean and fresh in his lungs. There was only a slight bite in the breeze today. A good sign. Winter was still a few weeks off.

As he turned onto Market Street, the heavy traffic demanded his complete concentration. Vendors, merchants and horse-drawn carriages formed a labyrinth of chaotic activity.

It was all so familiar. And yet, something felt… wrong. The hair on the back of his neck stood at attention, much as it had when he'd picked up Miss O'Toole this morning and noted her change in mood.

Shane was a man who dealt in facts, not feelings. Thus, he drew his horse to a stop outside his building and willed the sensation to pass.

Climbing down, he grabbed his medical bag and scanned the area. Nothing seemed out of the ordinary. Except…

A tall, brown-haired gentleman, dressed in a well-designed suit stared at him from across the street. Shane hadn't seen that sort of man since his youth, and only when he'd ventured beyond the Bowery to the more expensive neighborhoods of New York.

The man looked like a solicitor, or maybe a big-city banker. Or whatever he was, he certainly didn't belong in Denver.

Bothered that the sight of a stranger could disturb him so easily and wanting to return to Charity House as quickly as possible, Shane broke into a swift trot to avoid a fast-moving carriage and entered his office with a frown. The room stood empty, the air heavy and stuffy. A good cleaning was long past due but it would have to wait until the crisis at Charity House was under control.

Thoughts of the orphanage reminded Shane of his promise to check on Lizzie for Miss O'Toole.

Gathering the necessary supplies he would need for later, he grabbed the Charity House record book off the shelf and headed out.

Once back on the street, he gazed around him, pleased to discover the man in the stylish city clothes was no longer in the immediate area.

Ten minutes later, Shane only had to knock once before the big double doors of Mattie's brothel swung open. Although too early for any real activity, there were a few men taking their lunch break with the girls.

Before Shane could see what was what, or rather who was who, Mattie sidled up to him, grinning like a tomcat over his next easy prey.

"Well, well. Dr. Shane. Isn't it a little late in the day for you?" She craned her neck to glance around him. "Is your lovely opera singer with you?"

Shane's gut tightened at the calculating glare in her eyes. "There's been a breakout of measles at the orphanage," he said. "*My assistant* is tending the sick children."

"What a good girl. You tell her I asked about her."

When speaking of Miss O'Toole, Mattie had a softness about her around the edges that scared Shane spitless. "Don't try to recruit her."

Mattie tossed her hair over her shoulders and hitched her hip against his. "Shame on you, doctor, I wouldn't think of such a thing."

Yes, you would. "She's mine, Mattie."

A rush of satisfaction flicked in her eyes. "Is she now?"

"I meant, she's *my* assistant. Leave her alone."

"Right. Right." She bumped her hip against his again. "I know what you meant."

Frustration sent a growl humming in his throat. "I'm here to check on Lizzie."

Mattie's eyes filled with delight. Then she smiled. "She's over there." She waved her hand toward the center of the room.

Shane's stomach dropped. Just as Mattie indicated, Lizzie reclined on a red-velvet divan. Her shaking fingers held a champagne glass none too steady, the golden liquid swishing precariously close to the rim. Worst of all, she was entertaining a gentleman in every wrong sense of the word.

Disgusted, Shane swallowed back a wave of condemnation. He shouldn't be surprised. After all, this wasn't the first time he'd seen a woman on the verge of death one day resort to using her feminine wiles on a customer the next.

But now that the initial shock was wearing off, he rounded on Mattie. "What is Lizzie doing out of bed? Are you that heartless?"

Mattie jerked her chin at him. "Don't blame this on me. She made her choice."

"Did you pressure her?"

"Of course not." Clearly offended, her eyes hardened. "She won't do me any good dead, now will she?"

She was right. But Shane still narrowed his eyes in warning. "You will see she doesn't overtax herself," he said.

A pall of silence passed between them. "I'm not her keeper. She chooses to be here, Dr. Bartlett. As do the rest of my girls."

Her eyes were blank, almost lifeless, but Shane heard the resignation in the madam's voice, reminding him that desperate circumstances brought women like Lizzie to Mattie's doorstep. The madam offered them an answer to starvation, and for some, even a better life than what they'd experienced before, but that didn't make what she did right.

Prepared to do a little preaching, he opened his mouth but a soft, youthful voice caught his attention and he turned toward the sound. At the sight before him, he sucked in a hard breath. Annabeth, the young girl he and Miss O'Toole had met two weeks ago in Mattie's kitchen, carried a tray of long-stemmed glasses, weaving her way among the clientele. Every few feet she would stop and offer a flute of sparkling liquid to one of Mattie's patrons.

"What's she still doing here?" A burning throb of anger knotted in his throat. "I thought you told Beau she was a distant relative visiting for a week."

Mattie's eyes frosted to a cold, sharp blue. "You leave her out of this."

Their stares locked, clashed, but Shane refused to back down. "Who is she?"

"None of your business."

"She's too young to live in a brothel."

"I know that." She wrapped her arms around her waist in an uncharacteristic display of defensiveness. "She will return to boarding school as soon as the arrangements are made."

Something in the madam's eyes told Shane this was a personal matter for her, one he should leave alone.

He pushed anyway. "She attends a school back East?"

Mattie's expression closed, and he knew she was through answering his questions. "Let me remind you, Dr. Bartlett, your job is to care for the sick. Nothing more. Forget that, and you won't be allowed in my establishment again."

Her threat sent another burst of anger rolling through him, but he didn't doubt she meant every word. Business always came first for Mattie Silks. And aside from kidnapping Annabeth himself, there wasn't much he could do to help the girl. He had to trust that Mattie spoke the truth.

Shane released a frustrated sigh.

A breakout of disease, a stranger in town that left him feeling uneasy, a battle with a notorious madam over a young girl's fate, clearly, the day was shaping up to be one of his worst in years.

Chapter Twelve

Bella had never felt so helpless in her life. These children, these *innocent* boys and girls were in severe pain and she could do nothing of consequence to ease their suffering.

The letter from William was burning a hole in her pocket, but she didn't dare take it out now. There would be time when she was alone. Perhaps once the children went to sleep she would read what Lord Crawley had to say to her.

In the meantime, she wrung out a rag and brought it to Kimberly's heated forehead. "Does that help any?"

Kimberly closed her eyes and sighed. "A little."

Bella moved through the room and replaced the compresses on the other four girls' foreheads. Now that Dr. Shane had returned from town, he and Bella had decided to split the rooms between them. There hadn't been time to discuss anything else, since four more sick children had been sent home from the school.

According to the doctor's records, there could be another six still to come.

Bella caught a movement in the doorway.

She turned in time to see Dr. Shane motioning her into the hall.

Confused by his sudden appearance, she made her way quickly across the room. The moment she shut the door behind them she noted the lines of fatigue around his mouth and eyes. The man had to be exhausted, living with little sleep and meager wages, yet he never complained. His dedication awed her. Inspired her. Made her want to be a better person.

"You wanted to see me?" she asked.

"How are the girls?"

"Sick, hurting, bored. I'm afraid the bored portion of that equation is making them cranky."

Reaching out, he touched her sleeve and then just as quickly dropped his hand. "We'll get through this. A few days after the rash disappears the contagious period ends and then you will be able to return to your brother's home."

She thought of the two girls that had joined her room this afternoon, neither of which had shown any signs of rashes. "Are you saying you want me to stay here until the threat is over?"

"It's the best solution." He cocked his head at her. "Is there a problem with that?"

"No." Resigned at this point, she merely shook her head. "I was thinking about our other patients."

"I saw Lizzie today."

Bella didn't like the look in his eyes. "You have bad news."

"She's back to work."

Her eyebrows scrunched together at the news. "You don't mean—"

"I'm afraid I do." There was such sadness in his eyes, such loss, as though the idea of Lizzie returning to work was his own personal failure.

Bella understood completely.

"What a mess," she whispered. "If only I could speak to Mattie."

"It was Lizzie's choice."

"Yes, but—"

"Bella," he said with such gentleness she only half realized he'd used her given name. "The hard reality of life is that some people don't want to be saved. They're happy in their choices."

Why did she sense he was speaking from personal experience? Or had he seen into her heart and was urging her to change her ways?

"I thought she wanted to change." Was she speaking of Lizzie now, or herself? "She—"

"—is a prostitute."

This time, Bella didn't appreciate his harsh honesty. "By profession, maybe. But it's not who she is."

"For some, what they do *is* who they are."

He sounded so certain that tears of frustration filled her eyes. She swiped at them with the back of her hand.

"Lizzie's too weak for that kind of life. I have to go to her. I can talk sense into her, I know I can."

He stopped her with a firm grip on her arm. "You've been exposed to measles."

"But I've already had the disease."

"What if you're carrying the virus?" He released her arm. "You could infect Lizzie."

"I—"

With gentle fingers, he touched her cheek. "You know this, Bella."

Closing her eyes, she offered up a swift prayer for Lizzie's soul but the inability to help her friend left a sour taste in her mouth. "Oh, Shane, I feel so powerless."

He gave her a sad smile. "Now you know how I feel every day of my life. But then, our lack of control leaves us with the choice to open the door to God."

She shook her head at him. "Still…what an awful burden to carry, day in and day out. How do you manage it? All by yourself?"

"I'm not alone, Bella. Not anymore." He tentatively took her hand in his. "God answered my prayers. I have you now."

"Yes." She tightened her grip and smiled when a definite flash of contentment settled on his face. "Yes, you do."

Later that night, Bella waited until her patients had fallen asleep before settling down to read William's letter. The room was silent other than the soft snoring of the girls with stuffy noses.

Restless, Bella rose from her chair and moved to the window. Pressing her forehead against the cool glass, she studied the clear night sky. Black fabric strewn with a thousand diamonds, painted with God's skillful hand. Controlled chaos. Much like her life had become these last few weeks.

But unlike God's perfect masterpiece in the sky, Bella doubted she could hold on to her control much longer. Her secret was burning a hole in her soul, turning her conviction of sin into self-loathing. And her attraction to Shane Bartlett was confusing matters further.

Clutching William's letter in her hand, she could no longer put off the inevitable.

Returning to her chair, her hands shook as she slid a finger under the seal. Her pulse thundered loudly in her ears and she set the letter down in her lap.

What if William renewed his suit?

What if he didn't?

Taking a deep breath, she shifted until light from the moon illuminated the paper, flipped open the letter and read…

My dearest love, my Bella, my heart,

You were very naughty to run away from me. However, I do believe I understand. I am dreadfully sorry for the clumsy way I made my initial offer of protection to you. Come home at once and allow me to renew my suit properly. The arrangements

*are made. All you need do is contact my agent in
Denver and you will be on your way home to me.*

*Yours most affectionately,
William*

Come home? Renew his suit? "What of your wife,
William? *What of your wife?*" she hissed in the darkened room.

A rage so strong, so refined burned in Bella's chest
at William's callous arrogance, at his assumption a few
words scribbled on fine parchment would change her
mind and entice her down a road of sin with him.

How could he expect that of her? How could he?

A knock came at the door just as she crumpled the
letter in her fist. Confused by the distraction, she took
a deep breath and stared straight ahead. Still a bit disoriented, she looked around her. Blinked. Her gaze
landed on Stacy breathing heavily in her bed.

Another knock split through the silence.

Blowing out a heavy sigh, Bella jammed the letter
into her pocket and padded silently to the door. Ordering
her heartbeat to slow, tucking her rage into a dark corner
of her mind, she cleared her features and opened the
door a tiny crack.

Shane stood on the other side, carrying a tray with full
tea service. The skin beneath his eyes was dark with fatigue
yet there was contentment in his gaze. This was a man who
knew who he was, a man who understood his purpose in

life. He wasn't idle, like William, or confused over right and wrong. Shane Bartlett was good and sure and true.

Staring into his handsome face with those intense blue eyes and disheveled hair, Bella's earlier rage over William's letter shattered into something else entirely. Something far more pleasant. A tinge of hope sprang to life inside her.

She quickly lowered her gaze to the tray he carried. "What is this?" Her voice cracked a bit but he didn't seem to notice.

"You didn't eat much at dinner. I thought you might like some tea before going to bed."

The dear, dear man. Even in his own exhaustion he had thought of her. Again, something pleasant tugged at her heart. Not chaos, not fear, but something more refined, something comfortable and safe.

He smiled at her, a flash of white teeth and sincerity. "I'll set the tray in the upstairs parlor down the hall."

Not wanting to be alone with William's letter, Bella placed her fingertips on the doctor's forearm. "Will you join me?"

Lowering his gaze to her hand, he stared for a long moment and then nodded slowly. "I suppose it would be all right. As long as we leave the door open."

At the innocent announcement, memories assaulted Bella. Her mind sped back to the months of William's pursuit. She thought of the way he'd always closed the door to her dressing room during their visits. He'd claimed he hadn't wanted to share her with anyone, especially not the other members of her cast and crew. At the time, she'd thought his explanation sweet. Now she saw how dishonorable his actions had been.

She glanced over her shoulder at the girls, saw that they were asleep and slipped out the room. Vanity had her turning back. "I'll only be a moment."

Rushing to the mirror, she took a quick look at herself and cringed. Her hair was a tangled mess atop her head. Her face was lined with worry and exhaustion. William's locket looked cheap against her skin.

No one in London would recognize her. Oddly enough, that didn't seem such a bad thing at the moment. Of course, it would be ridiculous to try to tidy herself at this point. Dr. Shane had already seen her in this state and had agreed to share her tea anyway.

For a moment, a very brief moment, Bella's heart opened and she allowed herself to trust. To believe healing would come in spite of her mistakes.

It was a nice thought to end an otherwise horrendous day.

Chapter Thirteen

Unsure how long his assistant would take to join him, Shane rubbed an impatient hand down his face. The day had been a trying one, but ever since his connection with Miss O'Toole in the hallway he hadn't felt as weary as he might if he had to face this outbreak of measles alone.

There was no denying he and Miss O'Toole worked well together. And yet, he'd be foolish to forget that she held a portion of herself back. Foolish to hope more was growing between them than a healthy give and take of doctor to assistant.

Needing to walk off his uneasy mood, he rose but she joined him in the parlor at the same moment and he sat back down. She looked tired, a bit disheveled, yet incredibly beautiful. He decided she must be glorious on the stage.

Lowering herself in the seat opposite his, she shuffled around the cups on the tea service and began pouring.

Her movements were elegant, graceful, but he could tell something was bothering her tonight, more so than usual.

Was he pushing her too hard? Was she having regrets about agreeing to assist him? "Miss O'Toole, are you—"

"I realize I know so little about you, Shane. I can call you Shane, can't I?" She tossed her hair back and stared at him, those big tawny eyes of hers filled with anticipation.

Realizing she wasn't going to talk about herself, not yet at least, he eased back in his chair and nodded. "I believe we've progressed past the customary formalities."

"So, *Shane.* Did you grow up here in Denver?"

He carefully considered how to respond to her question. He went with the short answer. "I'm from back East."

A charming smile spread across her lips. "I knew it."

"Is that right?" She seemed a little too pleased with herself.

"Your accent. Very highbrow. You clearly come from money."

He didn't know whether to laugh or scowl at her incorrect observation. If only she knew the truth of his nefarious beginnings. But instead of sketching out the ugly details of his childhood, he said, "I was given the best education available in this country."

"Oh? Which schools did you attend?" she asked, her eyes filled with simple curiosity.

His heart tripped. For a second he thought of his mother. How she had longed for a better life for him than the one she'd given him in the Bowery. Her death had provided for his future in an unexpected way. "A premiere boarding school at first. Princeton next. Harvard Medical School."

"Ah." Sipping from her cup, she stared at him over the rim. "Do you have any family left back there?"

Unbridled emotions buzzed in his head like angry mosquitoes. He should have expected the question, prepared for it at least. "My mother is dead. She died when I was sixteen."

"I'm so sorry." Holding his gaze with a sympathetic look, she set her cup on the table and clasped her hands in her lap. "I can't imagine losing mine. She's my rock."

Silence hung between them. His mind blurred with complicated sensations, severing his ability to respond.

"Was your mother all you had, then?" she asked.

Shane sucked in a violent breath. Pride battled with weariness. Weariness won. He was tired of holding his past a secret. He needed to share his history. And he needed to share it with this woman. "I have a father and two younger sisters, two *half* sisters."

"I don't understand." She cocked her head at a charming angle. "Are you saying your father remarried?"

He held back a snort of disdain. "No. He only married once." Years of resentment sounded in that single word. "I'm a bas—that is, my father was never married to my mother."

A look of horror filled her eyes. "Does that mean—"

"My mother was a rich man's mistress."

Bella had an instant of pure shock. Her hand flew to her throat and her fingers knotted in the gold chain around her neck. She tugged, but only managed to tangle her hand further around the locket. Cutting through her shock was a quick, primal urge to run.

"I see I've rendered you speechless." His voice was flat, calm, but his eyes told her she'd let him down with her stunned reaction.

He didn't understand. He thought she'd judged him and found him wanting. But he was wrong. So. Very. Wrong.

The thought of this man, this kind, considerate healer, experiencing such a terrible childhood broke her heart. She freed her fingers from William's locket at last and reached to Shane across the small table between them. When he didn't shake her hand off his arm, she asked in a gentle voice. "Did you know your father? Was he part of your life at least?"

He relaxed into her touch, and she could see some of the tension easing from his shoulders. "My father never recognized me. Not in public, anyway."

"Oh, Shane." She squeezed his arm gently. "That must have been hard."

He made a low sound of anger in his throat, but he placed his hand calmly over hers. "When I was young, he came to see my mother weekly. But his visits decreased once I turned ten, stopped altogether when I was fourteen."

Bella had no words. Afraid she would say the wrong thing she rolled her palm against his, clutched tightly and then moved around the table to kneel in front of him.

How could she tell him she had a sick fascination with his tale, a personal interest that went far beyond curiosity?

So many thoughts ran through her mind.

At the time William had made his proposal, she had thought only of his wife as the victim. But what if Bella had accepted his proposition? Would she have had a child, like Shane's mother?

Her heart clenched in her chest. "How did your mother take your father's abandonment?"

"Badly. She died two years later, when I was sixteen." He shook his head. "But in truth, she died in her heart the day his visits stopped."

Words of sympathy seemed inadequate. So she pulled his hand to her face, laid her cheek against his palm.

He didn't register her touch, just stared into the distance. "My father must have heard of her passing because he came three days after her funeral. There'd been no sadness in him at the loss of a woman he'd claimed to have loved. *Love.*" He spat out the word. "Peter Ford didn't know the meaning of the word. He allowed my mother to suffer ridicule, shame and condemnation because of him. That's not love. That's possession."

"Yes." Her fingers curled around his wrist. *"Yes."*

"Instead of sharing his condolences, the man had the nerve to offer to pay for my education." Shane's bitter tone told her he hadn't considered the offer a blessing. Thus, his next words shocked her all the more. "I accepted."

"You…you did?"

"Not out of gratitude." His eyes blazed with distant memories and he pulled his hand away from her face. "I accepted out of revenge."

How could she fault a sixteen-year-old boy his anger? "You were young, Shane."

"There's more."

Still on her knees, she blinked up at him.

"There were…stipulations."

The raw pain in his eyes gripped at her heart. Bella had to help him understand she wasn't judging him. On the contrary, she was judging his father. His mother, even, for her inability to put her son ahead of her love for a wicked man.

A wave of tenderness had her pushing a clump of hair off his forehead. "What did he ask in return for your education?"

"I had to keep silent about my mother and my relationship to my father." His gaze filled with wounded pride. "In the eyes of the school administrators, I was a charity case of the great philanthropist Peter Ford."

"How that must have hurt. I'm so sorry."

"I agreed to the lie. I perpetuated it for my own end." His voice was husky with self-directed anger. She knew all about that particular emotion.

But, unlike her, he was wrong to condemn himself. "You were sixteen, alone and grieving your mother. You were vulnerable. Your father took advantage of that."

His spine went rigid. "I wanted revenge, not an education. In the end, I won."

Understanding dawned. "Instead of staying in New York you came here, to Denver, and opened a practice that caters to women like your mother."

His lips twisted in self-disgust. "A sinful, self-serving response, don't you think?"

"No, Shane. You might not realize it, but the Lord

brought you here, not your drive for revenge. Like Paul says in Romans 8, *God works for the good of those who love Him, who have been called according to His purpose.*" She cupped his face in her palms. "No matter how or why you came to Denver, you are living out your purpose for the Kingdom now."

"How can you be so sure? God wants our efforts to be out of a cheerful heart. I can't say that's true of me."

"Oh, but it is." Her affection for him felt so foreign, and yet so right. "You forget. I work alongside you daily. I see your strength of character, your integrity, your love for the lost. It's in everything you do. You save lives, Shane."

"Except my mother's life, she—"

"Your mother chose to love a married man. She chose to believe his lies."

Who better than Bella to understand the woman's delusions? She herself had chosen to believe William's false promises. She'd ignored the signs. She'd only been spared a life like Shane's mother through escape, not strength of character.

Her hand went to the pendant around her neck, her albatross.

"I couldn't save her," he whispered. "I failed my mother."

Bella dropped the locket. "No. Like you said when we were discussing Lizzie, there was nothing you could do. Your mother didn't want to be saved."

But Bella did. Oh, yes, Bella did.

She wanted to break free of William. Somehow, someway, she would find the courage to move forward with her life. If not in her own strength, then with God's help.

Why hadn't she seen the truth sooner? She had to let God take the lead. If her Heavenly Father could place stars in the sky, surely He could guide her through the process of repentance.

Only then would she be worthy of a man of Christian integrity, a man like this compassionate doctor who had turned his drive for revenge into something powerful for God's Kingdom.

Could she be falling for Shane Bartlett? Was that possible when she was still confused over her feelings for William?

As soon as the thought surfaced, Bella realized nothing would come of the situation.

One day Shane would find out about William. He would discover Bella had nearly thrown her life away over a married man, just like his mother had done.

And then he would hate her.

Shane watched the myriad emotions cross Bella's face. He saw understanding, pain, but not pity. How could someone so young and with such a small amount of worldly experience not judge him or his mother?

Because she was special. "I...thank you for listening, Bella. I've never shared that much of my past with anyone."

"No?"

"My half sisters know nothing of me. I was sworn to secrecy and I have kept to that vow."

Her gaze filled with sorrow. "You've carried this burden alone all these years?"

"Yes."

She slid back into her chair, studied his face intently. "Do you think you will ever forgive your father?"

It was a good question, an astute question, one he wrestled with daily. Looking into her intense gaze, he realized his answer mattered to her.

Was she expecting him to make the right decision, the godly one? If so, she was going to be sorely disappointed.

He knew what Jesus taught about forgiveness, had studied the Bible for hours while searching for freedom from his burning resentment. Unfortunately, Shane's hatred for the man who had fathered him ran too deep. And so he answered her question with complete honesty. *"Never."*

She nodded. "I…don't blame you."

Her quick response gave him a sick feeling in the pit of his stomach. And then, an ugly thought reared. Was Bella's secret, the one that made her eyes sad and kept her out of church on Sunday mornings, tied to an illicit association? Had she fallen for a married man? Was she pining for him now?

Shane prayed he was wrong. For both their sakes.

Chapter Fourteen

The quarantine lasted one week. Bella spent her last morning at the orphanage helping the girls dress for school.

Their excitement was so contagious she couldn't bear to stifle their fun. Thus, she allowed face scrubbings to turn into splashing and hair braiding into giggling.

With most of the girls already downstairs, Bella stood behind Stacy and secured a light blue, polka-dot ribbon atop her shiny brown curls. "There," she said, looking at their shared reflections in the mirror. "Perfect."

Getting into the spirit of things, Stacy spun around and twirled the skirt of her green dress. "You mean, perfectly mismatched."

"Precisely."

They giggled together but then Stacy's eyes turned serious and she threw her arms around Bella's neck. "Thank you, Miss Bella. Thank you for everything."

Heart in her throat, Bella hugged the girl tightly
against her. "It was my pleasure."

Which was nothing short of the truth. Thanks to her
constant days and nights with the children, Bella had
lost her uneasiness around them.

Peering over the top of Stacy's head, Bella eyed one
of the Scriptures scrolled along the wall. *Love each other
deeply, because love covers over a multitude of sins.*

The verse struck at her core. Love. Thanks to the
Charity House orphans, and a certain dedicated doctor,
Bella was learning a lot about the elusive emotion. And
none of what she discovered remotely resembled what
William had callously offered her.

One last squeeze and she released Stacy.

Casting her gaze around the room, her curiosity got the
best of her. "Stacy, do you know who painted these walls?"

"I did," said a soft voice from behind them.

Bella whipped around and connected her gaze with
a tall blonde standing in the doorway. She'd only met
the girl once, but even in that brief exchange Megan had
left an impression on Bella. More woman than child, the
kind look in her sea-green eyes spoke of a tender heart
and a gentle soul.

"You've done a lovely job here." Bella swept her
hand in an arc through the room. "Simply exquisite."

"Thank you." Megan smiled, but something sad came
and went in her eyes.

Bella recognized that look. The young woman was
suffering some sort of loss, but she was putting up a
brave front nonetheless.

"You're very talented," Bella added.

Megan lifted a shoulder then focused on Stacy. "Laney sent me to get you. You're late for breakfast. Johnny is already on seconds."

Stacy's face lost a few shades of color. "You don't think we'll run out of food?"

"Of course not." Patting her back, Bella handed the girl her coat. "But that doesn't mean you should dally up here any longer."

Stacy grabbed the garment and rushed into the hallway.

Smiling, Bella turned a circle and tried not to cringe at the mess she and the girls had made. Squaring her shoulders, she began picking up wet towels and blankets. Megan quickly joined her and they worked in silent harmony.

Bella had so many questions she wanted to ask the talented girl. Unsure how to begin, she set a blanket on the edge of a bed and looked at the walls again. "Have you thought of getting further training for your art? At a woman's college, perhaps?"

Megan's mouth opened and closed three times before she finally managed more than a squeak. "I could never leave Charity House."

"Because of money?"

Megan shook her head. "Nothing like that."

Bella took Megan's hand and drew her down on the bed. "I don't know you, and you certainly don't know me, but I must tell you that I think it would be a mistake to ignore your God-given gift."

"It's not that special. I was just having a bit of fun."

Megan sat stiffly as she spoke, oblivious to the beautiful world she had created with a vivid imagination and a paint brush.

"Are you afraid?" Bella asked, touching a hand to the girl's shoulder.

Grimacing, Megan stood abruptly. "Of course not."

Bella tugged her back down beside her. "The world isn't as frightening as it seems."

"I know." But she shifted out of Bella's reach and stared at her with eyes a frigid, pale blue.

"Megan, *please,* tell me what's keeping you here."

The girl rose, but didn't move, didn't blink. Bella feared she would stand there frozen forever, but eventually her face crumbled. "I can't…I can't risk losing him."

Bella's heart played a rhythmic beat against her ribs. "Him?" *Please, don't let her say Shane.*

"Logan. Logan Mitchell."

Relief swam in Bella's brain at the unfamiliar name. "I don't think I know him."

Megan twisted her fingers together in front of her. "He used to be Marshal Scott's deputy. He was transferred to the San Francisco office."

"I see."

Megan turned her head away, jaw set. "He will come back for me."

Ah, so Megan was yet another hopeful woman waiting for a man to fulfill his vow. How Bella wanted the girl's trust in Logan Mitchell to be warranted. But she bit her lip and resisted the sympathy building in her. One of them had to be practical. "How do you know he's coming back?"

"Because he promised. And I'll be here when he returns because *I* promised." Megan's sad sweet smile broke Bella's heart.

Such faith. Such blind trust. But at what cost? "Surely Marc and Laney would tell him where you were if you left to pursue your art."

The girl hugged her arms around her waist. "I won't have him misunderstand if I'm not here."

"But you have no idea when he'll return. It could be years."

"Then I'll wait years."

"Oh, Megan." What else could Bella say? The girl was so young, not yet twenty. How could Bella explain the harsh reality of a world she was only discovering herself?

"It was nice talking to you, Miss Bella." Megan looked toward the door as though it were an escape route. "But I need to check on the babies."

Bella didn't try to stop the hasty exit. But as she watched the girl leave the room frustration had her rising from the bed and balling her hands into fists.

Was this the same helpless emotion Shane had experienced as a child? How utterly and completely awful.

Her heart bled for the little boy Shane had been.

Unfortunately, she knew empathy could not change the past. That didn't mean Bella couldn't do something about the future.

Yes, she would do…something. Soon.

She just didn't know what. And she didn't know when. But details like that had never stopped her before.

* * *

The air in Shane's office pulsed with the scent of iodine, furniture polish and sulfur. Not particularly pleasant, but the room smelled exactly like a medical office should. Sadly, though, the familiar odors did nothing to calm Shane's restlessness. Ever since he'd revealed the details of his childhood to Bella, he couldn't relax around the woman. Even now, as they worked side by side preparing for their day, he had to tamp down his rambling thoughts.

Problem was, the woman knew too much about him now.

She hadn't spoken of the matter, nor had she tried to encourage further discussion, but for the last week, she'd gone beyond her normal duties. She kept his office tidy, ensured he ate three meals a day and never once allowed him to forget his coat.

Pondering the change in their relationship, Shane dumped a salicylic compound in a medium-size mortar and began mixing a fresh batch of painkillers.

With every few flicks of his wrist he cast a quick glance at Miss O'Toole. Dusting the bookshelves, the only sound she made was her gentle humming. Shane wondered what she was like on stage, singing the lead in some famed opera.

No doubt, she was stunning. Unforgettable.

Displeased with the direction of his thoughts, Shane set the pestle down and raked a hand through his hair, tugging at the ends as though he could yank his thoughts under control with the gesture. He couldn't forget Bella would soon be leaving. The reminder made his gut curl into a tight ball of dread.

Thankfully, a loud knock at the door splintered his musings.

Bella quit humming and settled her velvety eyes on him. "Do you want me to answer that?"

"No. Finish your dusting." He slanted his head toward the bookshelf. "I'll let you know if we have a patient."

She nodded, but instead of returning to her duties, she watched him move across the room.

Hand on the knob, a wave of foreboding washed over him and Shane hesitated, oddly reluctant to admit whoever was waiting on the other side.

Nevertheless, he threw open the door.

Blinking into the bright morning sun, his gaze landed on a complete stranger. Much older than Shane, the man was dressed in a tailored suit, his white hair slicked back in the popular fashion of the day. His small, expressionless eyes put Shane instantly on guard. "May I help you?"

Before the man had a chance to answer, Shane lowered his gaze to the man's hand. He carried a small leather satchel made specifically for holding important documents. Shane had seen an identical case in his father's possession the day he'd come with his offer of education.

"Are you Shane Bartlett?"

"I am." Shane leaned forward to get a better look at the satchel. "And you are?"

"Ronald Wilson. I have come on a matter of grave importance."

Frowning at the melodramatic words, Shane stepped back and allowed the man to enter his office.

Shoulders rigid, Ronald Wilson strode into the room. His gaze swept the small sitting area and stopped on Bella.

Shane stepped between them. "This is my assistant, Miss O'Toole."

The man removed his hat and nodded. "A pleasure, miss."

With her usual politeness, she inclined her head slightly, but then her solemn gaze connected with Shane's. From the glint in her eyes it was clear she didn't trust the man.

Shane didn't either. Something wasn't right about Ronald Wilson. He was too slick, too polished and he carried the scent of "city" all over him.

Shane slid his hands into his pockets and watched the man walk through his clinic with a confident step. Shane had seen that sort of walk enough to recognize the look of money.

"Are you in need of medical services, Mr. Wilson?"

"No."

A brief pause. Then the man continued his inspection, turning in a half circle before moving to the wall of bookshelves.

Bella came to stand next to Shane. The gesture turned them into a unit, much like the time she'd boldly announced to her brother she was going to be a nurse.

Standing here now, her narrowed eyes never leaving Ronald Wilson, she looked small and fierce and incredibly sweet.

Shane's heart gave a swift kick.

"I don't like this," she whispered. "I don't like *him*."

Mr. Wilson turned at that last part, his stare locking onto Bella. Shane didn't appreciate the light of interest in the other man's eyes. Stepping forward, he shifted Bella behind him.

A look of understanding flashed across the other man's face and he nodded. The respect laden in the simple gesture threw Shane off balance.

"My assistant and I have a busy day ahead of us. Please state your business, sir."

Mr. Wilson gave another quick nod. "Certainly." He paused, looked at Bella. "Perhaps we should speak alone."

Shane thought he heard a soft growl come from Bella's lips. Of course, he was mistaken. He had to be mistaken. But when she gripped his elbow in a silent request to remain he knew he couldn't deny her.

"She stays."

Mr. Wilson inclined his head. With quick steps, he strode to a table in the middle of the room and set the leather satchel on top. "I'll get straight to the point."

"I would appreciate that."

"I'm afraid there's no easy way to say this." He rested his palms on the table and adopted an expression of sympathy. "Your father is dead."

A long moment passed, and then as if in a nightmare, dark, angry emotions linked together in Shane's mind. Shock, relief, regret, guilt. The violence of his sporadic emotions hit like a punch in his gut, a hard, ruthless punch that stole his ability to take a decent breath of air.

Bella's hand tightened on his arm. "Shane," she whispered. "You should sit. You…"

He didn't hear the rest of her words over his own muddled thoughts. Of all the scenarios he'd expected this morning, the news of his father's death was not one of them.

With quick movements, Bella dragged a stool across the room and then urged him to sit with a hard push to his shoulders.

Knees unbuckling under the surprisingly strong pressure, Shane collapsed into the seat and gazed up at her. She approached him slowly, placed a hand on his cheek. The concern in her eyes was palpable. "It's okay, Shane. Take a moment to accept this."

Shaking his head, Shane glared at the man who had brought this unexpected news. "When did he die?" He held up a hand to prevent the other man from answering right away. "I don't care how, or why, I just need to know when."

"Three months ago."

Three months. Three months and Shane had known nothing, had sensed nothing. That alone spoke of the relationship he'd shared with the man who had sired him.

Hatred, bitterness, rage, a legacy of dark emotions was all that had existed between father and son. But to what end? Peter Ford was dead and Shane would no longer have the opportunity to…to what? Further his revenge? Make amends? Forgive?

How could God forgive a man like Peter Ford? More confounding still, how could Shane?

He forced his emotions to the back of his mind and tried to focus logically on the problem before him.

One question arose. "Why this visit, Mr. Wilson? Why not send a telegram?"

Head bent over the satchel, the man sighed. "I was Peter Ford's personal solicitor. Due to the nature of his business and certain life choices he made in his youth, he wanted complete privacy for a number of matters."

"*Matters?* You mean me and the situation of my birth."

"Yes, Dr. Bartlett. That is precisely what I mean." Eyes still cast down, he flipped open the leather pouch's flap and dug his hand inside. "I have kept track of you through the years on your father's behalf."

The statement could mean a number of things, but the sympathy in Mr. Wilson's eyes eroded any delusion on Shane's part of a father keeping tabs on a beloved son. Whatever the reason Peter Ford had monitored Shane's progress through the years, it had not been out of love.

Shane drew in a sharp breath, jerked his knee up and down in agitation. He relaxed only when Bella's hands smoothed over his hair.

"I still don't understand why you're here now?" he said once he had his control back in place.

"I have come to explain your father's will to you."

"His what?" Shane jumped up so fast the stool went tumbling behind him. Bella's touch to his arm kept him from rushing forward.

"Go on, Mr. Wilson," she said for them both. "Tell us the rest."

"Dr. Bartlett, your father left you everything."

Shane let out a bitter laugh as he batted away the declaration with a contemptuous wave of his hand. "Impossible."

"It's true." The solicitor pushed a mountain of papers toward Shane. "However, there is a stipulation."

"Of course." Shane curled his lip in derision. But then he remembered the others. "My father had a wife, and two daughters. Did he leave his family nothing?"

"My client's wife died several years ago. As for his daughters," Mr. Wilson's eyes turned sad, making Shane wonder what the man's life had been like in constant service for a man like Peter Ford, "they receive nothing of your father's estate."

Nothing? Peter Ford's daughters, daughters raised in the height of privilege, would get nothing from their father? Shane struggled with the ugly realization of their instant poverty, fought to close his heart to what that meant. But he could not. He had two sisters left destitute. What kind of monster had his father been? "How old are they now?"

"Drusilla is fourteen, Elizabeth only ten."

"Who is caring for them? Where are they living? How are they taking this change in their circumstance?" He fired off the questions like bullets from a six-shooter.

Mr. Wilson took a bracing breath of air. "They are residing in my home at present, but not in the style they have previously known. With four daughters of my own, and my largest client dead, I am a man of limited means."

Stunned at yet another unexpected revelation, Shane readjusted his first impression of the man. Of course, now that he was the sole heir of his father's estate, he would have to decide what to do about his sisters. He would...

He would...

A burst of confusion took hold of him. There was too much information coming at him all at once. He needed air, needed a moment to think and organize his thoughts. He started for the door, but Bella stopped him.

"Shane, wait. The stipulation." She gave him a meaningful look. "You have to listen to the rest."

Shane halted, spun to glare at Mr. Wilson. "What is the stipulation?"

"The details are spelled out in your father's will." The solicitor pointed to the pile of papers he'd set on the table. "You should read every page carefully for yourself."

Shane waved a dismissive hand. "Summarize the important points."

Mr. Wilson sighed. "In order to receive your inheritance, you must legally change your name to Ford, return to New York and take on your role as your father's rightful heir."

The air in the room turned cold, heavy, closed.

Shane swallowed. "And if I refuse my inheritance? Will my sisters receive the money in my place?"

Mr. Wilson shook his head. "If you refuse, the entire estate will be sold and the proceeds will be distributed to Harvard Medical School for the sole purpose of research."

Bella gasped. "Are you saying the money won't even go to charitable organizations?"

"Not a penny."

With that simple statement, any remaining hopes

Shane might have had about his father's motives disappeared. Peter Ford had been a selfish, cold-blooded man in life, and was proving no better in death. And this time, with one swoop of the pen, the ruthless snake had found a way to control them all from his grave.

Chapter Fifteen

B ella had heard enough, but before she could expel the solicitor, Shane straightened to his full height and forced out a hard breath. "I think you should leave, Mr. Wilson. I need time to sort through everything you've told me."

With each word spoken, Shane held himself rigid, his gaze locked on the solicitor like a hunter eyeing his prey. His breathing wasn't quite steady and he looked upset. Bella went to him, touched his back. No, not upset, she decided. Furious. She could feel the rage in the bunched muscles below her palm.

"Mr. Wilson," she appealed, employing all the charm she could muster under the circumstances. "The doctor is only asking you to allow him the opportunity to study his father's will, as you yourself suggested a moment ago."

The solicitor lifted his left eyebrow the barest fraction but, mercifully, his eyes held a considerable amount of compassion in them. "I suppose a few days will make no difference one way or the other."

"Thank you for your understanding," she said, removing her hand from Shane's shoulder.

A muscle in his jaw flexed as he clenched his teeth. She could tell he was trying to contain his rage but the threads of his control were unraveling with every heartbeat.

With swift movements, Bella helped the solicitor gather his belongings and ushered him toward the door.

Hand poised above the knob, Mr. Wilson peered over his shoulder at Shane. "I will return Tuesday afternoon, if that meets with your satisfaction."

"Tuesday will be fine," he said.

Wanting the man gone, Bella placed a solicitous hand on the man's arm. "I thank you again."

After closing the door with a click, Bella took a long, slow, careful look around her. With so much information to take in, she decided to give Shane another moment to cool his anger. Flexing her fingers, she walked to the table where Shane's copy of the will sat. Unable to relinquish her awful fascination, she stared at the top page but the letters snaked into blurry, incomprehensible lines before her eyes.

Outraged on Shane's behalf, she lifted her gaze to his and found herself confronted with cold disdain. Even knowing his fury was not directed at her, she quickly lowered her head.

He'd held so much bitterness toward his father before this. *How will he find peace now, Lord?*

With legs that felt full of water, she made her way across the room. "Shane?"

Unblinking, he stared over her head. His stone-cold expression worried her. Why wasn't he ranting, yelling, showing some emotion, *any* emotion?

At last, his eyelids tapered to tiny slits. "He never accepted me."

She knew he meant his father. "He's left you his entire estate."

Shane gave one hard shake of his head. "With impossible limitations attached."

"Perhaps he thought he was doing the right thing."

Scowling, he pushed forward. His expression held the regret of a man who knew he would never achieve what he wanted most in life. "I was not a son to him. Even now, he only wants his name to live on through me." He clenched his jaw. "I was never able to earn his love."

In spite of his anger, Bella didn't miss the agony in his eyes, or the pain in his voice. "I don't have any fine words for you. And I don't have any answers. But I can steer you to my mother's favorite verse, one that has held me up in times of despair."

She hurried to the small round table next to one of the sickbeds in the room and retrieved the Bible Shane kept there. Her fingers shaking, she flipped to Isaiah 40 and began to read. "But those who hope in the Lord will renew their strength. They will soar on wings like eagles; they will run and not grow weary, they will walk and not be faint."

Shane furrowed his brow as he joined her. For a long

moment he stood next to her, unmoving, while he stared at the page. With an incomprehensible mutter, he took the Bible and concentrated on the passage she indicated with her finger.

Bella waited for him to speak. A dozen platitudes came and went in her mind. *Oh, Lord, if ever there was a time for the right words, this is it. Please guide what I say.*

"Shane, God's love is unfailing and unconditional. You might not have earned your earthly father's love but you will always have your Heavenly Father's love."

Unflinching, he stared at the page.

She touched his arm. "It's no accident God brought you here. The Lord will use this experience for good. He's been preparing you for a specific assignment all along. Remember, most of the children at Charity House have been abandoned by their fathers, just like you."

And still, he stared at the Bible. The only sign of his turmoil came in the fast ticking of a vein in his neck.

"Shane." She shook his arm. "What would your patients do if you weren't here? You yourself said no other doctor will see them. Who would care for them if not you? God had a plan for you from the start."

Closing his eyes a moment, Shane shut God's Word and returned it to the nightstand. "If I stay…" He pressed a finger to his temple. "What happens to my sisters?"

She gave him an overbright smile. "You could send for them."

"And how would I care for them?" He looked around him in disdain. "I can barely afford these rooms."

"I don't know." She shook her head. "Maybe—"

"Don't you understand?" His eyes hardened. "Peter Ford knew what he was doing when he put that stipulation in his will. He *knew* he was leaving me in an impossible situation."

"I—"

"If I stay here, continue as I always have, I abandon my sisters in the care of a stranger, one who readily admitted his funds are running low. Yet if I return to New York, I abandon my patients here."

Bella had no good argument. She had no answer at all. He was correct. Completely, utterly, miserably correct. A fresh spurt of defeat tickled her throat, but she would not allow Peter Ford to win that easily. "There's an answer, Shane. God already knows what it is. We just have to pray He'll reveal it to you soon."

After a brooding hesitation, Shane nodded. "Perhaps God does have a plan."

Despite his words, Bella saw the skepticism in his eyes. Shane wasn't agreeing with her. He was appeasing her.

Under the circumstances, there was only one thing left for her to do. She closed her eyes and began praying on his behalf.

At half-past eight the next morning, Bella threw out every lofty ideal she'd spouted to Shane in his office. She might have spoken of the power of prayer and the need to believe God already had a solution, but when it came to her own life she lacked the courageous faith she expected of Shane.

Some Christian she was turning out to be.

Oh, she knew all the right words, had memorized countless Scriptures, but when it came to her own troubles her actions had yet to reflect her beliefs. And as James said, what was faith without deeds?

Unwilling to have a lengthy conversation with Beau this morning, she silently tiptoed to the back door and found herself halting at a soft plea from behind. "Bella, please, don't run away like this."

Bella spun around, her eyes landing on Hannah standing stiffly in the kitchen doorway. Bella opened her mouth to rail at the unsolicited interference, but the genuine concern in her sister-in-law's eyes made the words back up in her throat. "Hannah, I'm not—"

"Don't deny it." Hannah glided closer. "Not to me."

Bella lowered her gaze to her toes. "I *must* check on Lizzie. It's been two weeks since I've been able to spend any time with her." She lifted her gaze. "I fear I've failed her."

"What of your other fear?"

Thanks to years of training, Bella mastered her emotions enough to give her reply without her voice shaking. "I have no other fear."

Brows knit tightly together, Hannah took a few steps forward and held out two more letters. "These came for you last week, the last one just yesterday."

Bella saw the familiar scrawl on the top envelope and backed up as though it were a snake ready to bite. William was her past, yet he was turning out to be her ongoing shame, as well. "I…no, I don't want them. Throw them out."

Flipping over the top letter, Hannah studied the fancy red seal. "He's very persistent."

Bella closed her eyes until the need to shudder passed. Unable to craft a good explanation, she lifted a pleading look to Hannah. "Please. Take them away from me."

Hannah sighed. "I can't. They are addressed to you. *You* must decide what to do with them." She placed the letters in Bella's palm and closed her fingers over the thick stack of papers.

Swamped by her churning emotions, Bella stuffed the offensive letters in her pocket and turned to go.

This time, a light touch to her shoulder stopped her progress.

"Bella."

Bella shrugged her off and pivoted to glare at her sister-in-law. "No. Don't."

Hannah lifted her hand to her hair, shifted a curl off her forehead. "What have I done to make you distrust me?"

Fists clenched, Bella fought back tears. "It's not you, Hannah. It's… You're too good."

Hannah's gaze softened and she gave a short laugh. "Oh, Bella. We all sin and fall short of the glory of God. Even me."

Bella saw the look of genuine sorrow on Hannah's face. Yet what had she done? Said a bad word? Forgotten to pray one morning? Certainly nothing of real consequence, nothing as bad as desecrating a marriage.

"I find that hard to believe." Her tone sounded bitter even to her own ears.

Hannah placed her palms in the air. "All right. We'll

leave it a little longer. But, Bella, know this." She tugged her into a tight embrace. "You can trust that I am here to listen whenever you need me."

And with those words, Bella felt worse. She'd been harsh and abrupt with her sister-in-law, yet Hannah still dealt with her in love. The woman personified the Fruit of the Spirit. Hannah would be a trusted confidant, but Bella couldn't find it in her heart to share her secret with her.

"I have to go." She rushed out the door without looking back. She heard Hannah's sigh of defeat right before the door banged shut behind her.

Less than a half hour later, Bella entered Mattie's brothel with determination in her steps. An eerie silence enveloped the main salon, but Bella hardly noticed. She wove her way through the open area, past the divans and chairs that had been full of paying customers the night before.

Instead of feeling out of place in this den of iniquity, Bella felt safe, protected. But whether that was due to the Holy Spirit's indwelling or a guilty conscience she couldn't say for sure.

One thing was certain, though, she understood the women who lived and worked in this house. Perhaps she had a connection with these women because she knew what it felt like to live with the blot of shame.

Deep in thought, Bella ascended the stairwell slowly. At the top of the landing she heard both male and female laughter coming from down the hall. Surely, a customer wouldn't visit this early in the day, not even on a Saturday? Would he?

Uncertain if she wanted to know the answer, Bella padded silently down the hallway and paused outside Lizzie's room. The laughter was coming from just inside.

Undaunted, Bella curled her fingers into a fist and knocked on the door.

The laughter stopped.

She knocked again. "Lizzie, it's me. Bella. I've come to read to you this morning."

No response.

She reached for the knob. "Lizzie? Are you in there?"

"Go away, Bella. I'm…working."

Bella snatched her hand back to her side. Her blood turned to ice. Shane had been right. Lizzie *had* returned to her old ways. "But, Lizzie, I—"

"Why, if it isn't Miss Bella O'Toole herself, just the girl I wanted to see."

Bella swung in the direction of the familiar voice, took a steadying breath. "Hello, Mattie."

Mattie nodded in response. Although still dressed from the night before, the madam's finely sculpted lips were unpainted, making her look less artificial and more approachable.

"Bella, darling, what are you doing up here all alone?"

Surprised at the question, she kept her tone light and friendly. "I was visiting Lizzie. Thought I'd read to her."

Mattie's gaze fused with hers so long Bella shifted under the blunt inspection.

"She wasn't expecting you this morning," Mattie said at last.

Bella's shoulders slumped forward. "I gathered as much."

The madam's eyes narrowed, then she nodded absently, as though she'd come to a conclusion of some sort. "Follow me. I have something to show you."

Oddly enough, as the woman took Bella's hand and tugged her down the hallway, her face held the same compassionate look as Hannah's had earlier. Bella didn't like the expression any better on the madam's round, overly powdered features than she had on her sister-in-law's. Nevertheless, she didn't struggle as Mattie literally dragged her down the back stairs.

Once inside Mattie's private parlor, Bella pulled her hand free. "What is it you wanted to show me?"

"Nothing." Mattie smirked. "I just wanted you out of the area."

Bella made a face. "Are you protecting me? Or Lizzie?"

Before responding, Mattie took her time reclining into a large, cushioned chair facing the door. "Why, you, of course."

Bella jammed her hands on her hips. "Isn't that a bit out of character, Miss Silks?"

"Perhaps." Mattie rose and ambled over to the bookshelf, pretending grave interest in the titles written on the spines. "Or perhaps I like that arrogant brother of yours and wanted to do him a favor."

"Try again, and this time why don't you play it with a little more feeling."

"Perhaps I simply like and admire you."

Rooted to the spot, Bella blinked in astonishment at the madam's declaration.

Seemingly unaware of the stunned silence, Mattie pulled out a book, studied the title and then put it in a new spot farther down the shelf.

Tapping her foot in impatience, Bella broke the silence between them. "You know, Mattie, I find it necessary to stomp on your illusions concerning me."

Mattie continued running her finger along a row of books. "How so?"

"Let's just say you wouldn't admire me if you really knew me."

"Secrets?" Mattie spun to stare at Bella. "I love secrets. And from one so young. My, oh my, I've struck gold."

Unsure what to make of the madam's strange response, Bella looked down at her hands, and because they refused to stop trembling, she folded them tightly around her waist. "Half your girls are younger than me."

"True. True. But none of them have a caring family to watch over them."

Bella took immediate offense, but refused to show it. She was Isabella Constance O'Toole. She knew exactly how to portray a woman of the world. Nevertheless, her hands still trembled as she lifted them to smooth her hair. "I'm not a child, Mattie. I've been on my own for two years now."

"So young. And jaded already." Returning to her chair, Mattie sank into the cushions with a soft whoosh. "Are you in trouble, dear?" She lowered her gaze to Bella's stomach.

Bella instinctively clasped her waist. "Of course not."

Mattie simply looked at her.

"All right, yes."

Mattie's eyes widened.

"Not *that* sort of trouble."

A sigh of relief was the madam's only response.

Feeling more than a little moody, Bella threw herself into the chair opposite Mattie's and proceeded to sulk for two entire seconds. But then she stopped herself. She was tired of thinking about William, about his ugly proposal and the newest batch of letters in her pocket. But most of all, she was just plain tired of *thinking*. Her secret was becoming too much to endure alone.

She hadn't been able to confide in Hannah, but Mattie was a woman who had made her share of mistakes. Mattie would understand. She would recognize the darkness inside Bella. Perhaps that explained why she blurted out, "I had a suitor in London."

Mattie chuckled. "I'd wager more than one."

"No, just one. But he was special. A viscount. I... He..." Bella rose, started pacing, halted just as quickly. "I thought he loved me. I thought he wanted to marry me."

Mattie's wise eyes stared into hers. "You were wrong, of course."

"He asked me to be his mistress." Bella buried her face in her hands. "I'm so ashamed. No. *No.* Not ashamed." She dropped her hands and pounded her fists in the air. "I'm angry."

"You gave in to him?" Mattie's question held no judgment, just curiosity. And maybe a little sympathy.

Bella threw herself back into her chair. "No."

"Then why all this anger?"

"I believed his lies, all of them, I never once doubted him, even when it was clear his stories weren't matching up with his actions."

Mattie laughed, a condescending sound that made Bella feel as if she was twelve years old again. "You think you're the first? Women are notoriously foolish in the face of pretty words and false promises. And I'm sure viscounts have their charm."

Bella's frustration rose, probably because she wasn't convincing Mattie of her obvious sin and resulting darkness in her soul. "You don't understand. He was married."

"You're not shocking me, dear." Mattie stretched out her leg and nudged Bella's foot with the toe of her shoe. "Any woman who looks like you is bound to have men fall in love with her. And for most men, marriage is not a deterrent in the face of such beauty."

Unimpressed with Mattie's summation, Bella scoffed at the ridiculous notion. "Marriage is sacred. No matter what anyone says, I know the truth. I ruined a marriage."

"I thought you said you didn't give in to him, so technically—"

"I was tempted. But instead of standing firm in my convictions, instead of refusing him outright, I ran away. I ran here."

Mattie gave her a funny look, glanced over her head and then released an odd, calculating smile. "Let me see if I have this straight." She tapped a finger against her lips. "A married man asked you to be his mistress but instead of accepting you ran to your brother for safety?"

The calmly spoken words hit Bella like a slap. "Don't you see? That makes me a coward."

"In my estimation," Mattie glanced up again, "that makes you the bravest person I know."

Bella snorted.

Mattie glanced over her head, *again*. "Do you still love this viscount?"

She thought of Shane then, how he treated her with respect and honor. She thought of his patience, his integrity. How he made her feel safe and important, and very, very special. With Shane she was simply Bella, a woman worthy of acceptance for herself. Not Isabella, the famed opera singer worthy of nothing more than a role as mistress in any man's life.

Mattie nudged her foot again. "You haven't answered my question. Do you still love your viscount?"

"I couldn't love a man who thought that little of me."

"That's not an answer."

Shrugging, Bella reached into the front pocket of her skirt. "William has been sending me letters, begging me to return to England and the cozy 'setup' he has planned for us. These latest ones, I can't open them. It would be a betrayal to Sha—" She cut her own words off before she revealed her heart. There were some secrets Bella would never reveal to Mattie, or anyone else.

Tight-lipped, she handed the letters to Mattie. "Will you dispose of them for me?"

Staring at the papers in Bella's outstretched hand,

Mattie remained firmly planted in her chair. "I'm confused. Who would you betray by reading those letters?"

"No one." Bella jabbed the envelope in the air between them. "Take them. Please."

At last, Mattie snatched up the letters and leaned back in her chair. "You're a brave girl, Bella O'Toole, but you can't hide your feelings as well as you think."

"What do you mean by that?" Bella snapped. She wasn't in the mood for one of the madam's infamous word games.

"You're in love all right." Mattie wagged the letters at her. "And I'd wager my house the viscount isn't the one holding your heart."

Bella gave a noncommittal shrug. Mattie saw too much. With a little encouragement she would turn Bella's feelings for Shane into something sordid.

Still grinning, Mattie glanced at a spot over Bella's head, again, the fourth time if Bella was counting. Which she was. *What was the madam up to now?*

Sensing they weren't alone anymore, Bella looked over her shoulder and saw Shane standing in the doorway.

Frozen inside her shock, she wanted to howl in outrage and then, *and then,* she wanted to snatch Mattie off her chair and shake her.

It was painfully clear what the ornery madam had been up to with all her questions of love. She had known Shane was standing behind Bella.

Marshaling as much grace as she could, Bella rose and turned to face Shane eye-to-eye. This was not a time for pleasantries, so she moved straight to the point. "How long have you been standing there?"

His stricken expression answered her question. "Long enough."

Chapter Sixteen

Shane didn't know what was worse. To discover Bella was yearning for a man she left behind in London or that she had shared her secret with Mattie Silks.

Either way, his greatest fear was realized. He'd fallen for a woman who longed for another man, just as his mother had pined for Peter Ford his entire childhood. And so the vicious cycle continued.

He turned to leave.

"Shane, wait."

He halted midstep but didn't turn back around. He couldn't look into her eyes now. Not with the knowledge of her love for another man standing between them.

He knew he had no right, but jealousy ran hot in his veins.

"Please." Her voice came out very small, very sad. "Let me explain."

For a maddening second, his heart pounded with expectation. But he gave a one-shoulder shrug and distanced himself from her with a step forward. "You owe me no explanation."

"Oh, but I do." He heard her footsteps approach. Then her hand touched his back. Her fingers felt like ice through his jacket.

Clearing her throat, Mattie moved to his other side. "I think I'll go check on, oh, I don't know…something."

She brushed past him, turned, then gave him an encouraging look wrapped inside years of experience. "Hear her out," she said, a bit misty-eyed. "You might be surprised what she reveals."

She squeezed his hand then hurried off. Shane could only stare in amazement. An infamous madam playing matchmaker? That was too much even for his open mind.

With great effort he turned on his heel and entered the room. With each step he took, Miss O'Toole backed out of his way. The trepidation in her eyes made him wonder if she was afraid of him, or frightened of what he might say.

Better and better.

"You have nothing to fear from me," he said. "I'm the last person to judge you."

Shame flooded her eyes and she bowed her head. "I never wanted you to know what brought me here."

"You mean…*who.*"

She visibly cringed. "Yes, who." Head down, she shuddered again. "But you must believe me when I say I didn't know he was married."

Neither had Shane's mother known Peter Ford was

married, at first. "What do you want me to say to you, Bella?"

Slowly, she lifted her head. Her eyes pleaded with him to understand, to forgive. "Tell me you don't hate me."

How could he? He was so far from that emotion his heart hurt. "I don't hate you."

She released a sigh. "But you think less of me."

Ah, a moment of truth. Dark emotions rose within him, anger so deep, so penetrating it battled with his hope for a future with this woman. Nevertheless, the truth could not be avoided, at least not in his own mind. He'd found a woman that made him want to risk love for the first time in his life. And he feared her heart belonged to another man.

No, he didn't judge her. He judged himself.

When he continued staring at her in silence, she shook her head. "Why are you so stoic? Tell me I'm bad, rant at me, call me a name."

"To what purpose?"

She rushed to him, gripped his hands. He hated how good her hands felt wrapped around his, hated how much he wanted to believe in her.

"I didn't give in to temptation, Shane. I ran. Isn't that worth something?"

"Yes, Bella, it is. But it doesn't matter in the end. All that really matters is what you do in the future." He took a deep breath and braced himself for the most important question of all. "Are you still in love with him?"

"No!"

He didn't believe her. She'd answered too quickly, as

his mother had always done when he'd held her head in his lap after she'd spent hours crying over Peter Ford.

He will come. He will come, she chanted over and over again.

He never did.

And then she'd say: it doesn't matter. *I don't love him. I don't love him.*

But she did.

"You don't believe me." Her hand flew to her throat and her fingers fiddled with the pendant around her neck.

Shane's heart went numb. "Did he give you that?"

She dropped the gold chain at once. "Yes, but I—"

Shane lifted a hand to stop the rest of her words. No matter what she said, if she still wore the man's necklace she still cared. "No, Bella, don't continue. I don't want to hear any more. I know. I *know* what this is about." He shut off all emotion. "I think it best I renew my search for a qualified assistant, beginning today."

Her eyes filled with tears. She swiped at them with the back of her wrist. "Are you dismissing me?"

"Yes."

"Have I done a poor job for you?"

"No. You've been competent." *Wonderful. Exemplary. An answer to prayer.*

"Don't hold this against me, Shane. Let me continue as your assistant. At least with your patients in the brothels and mining camps. I know I'm tainted, so I won't go near the Charity House children again."

Is that what she thought? That he was dismissing her because she was soiled? "It's not that, Bella. The children of Charity House have seen much worse in their own mothers."

"Then what is it? Why dismiss me now? You have so much on your mind not to accept my help. You need me to pick up some of the duties so you can work on a solution to your father's stipulation in his will."

His father's will. Shane had nearly forgotten about that ugly little mess. In the span of days, his past had come back to haunt him through both his dead father *and* his dead mother. But it was the hazy memories of his mother's hopeless face that gave him the courage to speak the truth. "You're right. I do need your help, but I can't rely on you indefinitely. Eventually you will leave and return to the stage."

"Please, Shane." She pulled his hand to her face, fitted his palm against her cheek. "Let me continue working with you." Her eyes asked for more from him.

Staring into her beautiful, shattered gaze he knew he would give in to her plea. Not because she asked it of him, but because he couldn't bear to say goodbye to her yet.

In that moment, sadly enough, he understood his mother better. He now realized how the smallest spark of encouragement could make a person act against logic. *I don't love her. I don't love her.*

But he did.

"All right, Bella. I will see you Monday morning as usual." He turned to go, but pivoted back around as a thought occurred to him. "And, Bella, for what it's worth." He paused, hesitant to continue.

"Yes?"

"Temptation is not the same as sin."

Her face crumbled. "Jesus taught that the thought is equal to the act."

"Yes, that's why the thought must be surrendered to the Lord the moment it occurs."

"What are you trying to say?" The flicker of hope in her eyes made him feel strong, powerful. He wanted to ease this woman's pain, a woman who would always love another man. What did that say about him? It said he was more like his mother than he wanted to admit.

"You haven't sinned, Bella." He held her gaze, willing her to hear what he was saying. "Not yet."

The next morning, Bella stood outside the Charity House church. Thanks to a sleepless night, her eyes felt gritty and every muscle in her body ached. But she would not use her physical discomfort as an excuse to avoid God any longer.

She had to stop running. And if she didn't attend church today, she feared she never would.

She fingered the locket around her neck. It felt heavy, like a shackle that couldn't be removed with a simple tug.

Lord, please help me walk through those doors. Help me to put You first today.

Maybe then, once she'd realigned her priorities in the proper order, she would be able to remove her gold-chained albatross. Yes. She was sick of her self-absorption, sick of allowing William's ugly motives to cause her any more shame. It was time to put her Lord first. Today, she would forget her past, forget her worries over Shane and simply worship her Father in Heaven.

As she began her ascent, each step became more difficult. To an outside observer her slow progress must look ridiculous.

She turned to leave. And came face to face with Shane.

"Going somewhere?"

"No, I… Yes. That is, I…"

"The entrance is facing the other way." His tone was incredibly gentle, the tone he used with his most frightened patients.

Could he read her panic? Did that mean he forgave her? Could one day make such a difference? Could she possibly think in anything other than a question?

"I—"

"Would you allow me to escort you inside?"

Glory…*glory,* but she saw genuine respect in his eyes, as though he knew how hard it was for her to enter God's House.

"Please."

Smiling, he placed his hand on her elbow and swung her around. With a quick repositioning, he tucked her arm under his and drew her closer to him.

She felt incredibly protected.

Best of all, he was still smiling.

Truly, the man was incredibly handsome when he smiled. The simple gesture softened all those sharp planes and angles. She cast a covert look at him from under her eyelashes. He was dressed in his usual uniform of black pants, black waistcoat and black jacket, but today his hair was pressed down in place. He looked far too handsome for a country doctor. *He'd put any leading man to shame.*

She was so caught up in studying Shane she almost forgot to be nervous about entering God's House. Almost.

The moment their feet crossed the threshold she wavered. He pulled her tighter against him. A show of solidarity, much like she'd done when they'd faced Mr. Wilson together in his office two days ago.

Bella relaxed. A little.

Shane led her to the back pew. As she settled in next to him, she folded her hands in her lap and looked straight forward.

She could do this.

Her hands started to tremble. *How* was she going to do this? Would people be able to read her sin in her eyes?

Did her iniquities show on her face?

Men and women, some familiar, some strangers, nodded at them as they passed by, but none made an attempt to sit in the pew with them.

Surely it wasn't because of her?

As though hearing her thoughts, Shane leaned toward her and spoke in a whisper. "I always sit in the back, in case I have to leave quickly. Part of being a doctor."

"Is that why no one joins you in this pew?"

He looked thoughtful for a moment. "I never thought about it, but yes, I suppose so."

People continued to file down the center aisle and Bella dared to watch the door to see who might show up today. She was quickly rewarded with the sight of the Scott family. Ten-year-old Molly led the way, marching quickly down the aisle, her head held high. Her father rushed after her, probably trying to ensure she didn't do something outrageous in the short distance to their seats.

Bella's father had done the same with her. Little Molly Scott was a girl after Bella's own heart.

Mrs. Scott walked slower, more serenely, with Ethan by her side. The little boy looked at Shane, peered around him and caught sight of Bella. He waved his hand and yelled, "Miss Bella! Hi, Miss Bella."

Bella waved back. "Hello, Ethan."

Over her shoulder, Katherine Scott smiled at Bella, nodded to Shane then stopped. She scooted Ethan forward and told him to join his father.

Satisfied her son was going to obey, she leaned over the adjoining pew and said, "I know this is an unusual time to ask, but would you two care to join us for Sunday dinner today? We haven't really had a chance to thank you for all you've done for Ethan and the Charity House orphans."

Bella sat up straighter. Sunday dinner with the Scott family? She wasn't sure she could take church and the quintessential, perfect family all in one day.

Shane looked to Bella, an encouraging smile on his face. "Do we dare?"

"I don't know. I—"

"Ethan would be devastated if you said no," Mrs. Scott added.

Bella relaxed. "Well, we wouldn't want to disappoint the poor boy."

"Is that a yes?"

Bella nodded slowly. "It's a yes for me."

The other woman lifted a brow at Shane. He grinned at her. She grinned back. Bella's stomach clutched. The two had a connection that she didn't quite understand. It wasn't exactly like brother and sister, but—

"Yes for me, too," Shane said over her thoughts.

Pleasure filled the other woman's eyes. "Wonderful." She swiveled around and continued toward her family.

Once everyone settled into their seats, Beau walked to the front of the church. As one, the congregation stood and opened their hymnals as he directed.

For a moment, Bella closed her eyes and allowed the words to wash over her. By the second stanza, she joined in the song. Immediately, her heart lifted with her voice and she focused all her praise on her good God this glorious day.

Sensing others staring at her, she opened her eyes and noticed the people closest to her sneaking glances her way.

"Am I singing too loudly?" she whispered to Shane.

He shook his head. "No." He squeezed her hand. "You're lovely. I mean…your singing is lovely."

All that intensity and emotion thrown her way gave her encouragement to continue. When the song was done, everyone sat.

Beau caught her eye, smiled and then gave her the big-brother look that meant he was about to challenge her to a dare.

Bella swallowed. *Oh, no, Lord, please no.*

"I have a treat for all of us. My sister has agreed to sing 'Amazing Grace' for us."

"I did no such thing," she muttered.

"You can do this," Shane said softly.

"No, I can't."

"You *need* to do this." He closed his fingers over hers. "Trust God."

Trust. Her breath turned frigid in her lungs. Why was it the big things in life always came down to trust?

Knowing Shane was right, she slowly rose and made her way to the front of the church.

All eyes were on her. Oddly nervous for a woman who had performed before packed houses, she kept her gaze glued to the pulpit straight ahead.

When she arrived at the front, Beau reached for her hand and gave her a triumphant smile full of brotherly love.

Feeling more confident, Bella turned to face the congregation. And then, in an attempt to gain the sisterly upper hand, she muttered a warning. "I will kill you for this."

"You're welcome to try."

"Don't think I won't."

Taking a deep breath, her gaze landed on Hannah's face. Tears spiked her sister-in-law's lashes. Tears of joy, tears of understanding.

Bella swallowed.

Hannah gripped Mavis's hand tightly and the two nodded at Bella with approval. It was the same look she'd seen in Shane's eyes when he'd encouraged her to accept her brother's challenge.

Refusing to look at any more faces, Bella began singing "Amazing Grace." The words flowed out of her memory, out of her soul. And with the declaration of her sinful nature, a sense of well-being filled her.

No more shame. No more guilt. Just a strong desire for repentance.

Shane's words returned to her. Temptation is not the same as sin. Her flesh had been tempted, but Bella had remained obedient to God.

All this time, she had thought she carried the burn of a scar, but she had learned from weeks as Shane's assistant that scars did not come with pain. Only wounds.

She needed to allow God to heal her wound.

And the process began with confession.

When she came to the last stanza she locked her gaze with Shane. His eyes were intense, unblinking and full of awe.

She held his stare and a tear slipped from her eye. Followed by another. After the third, she gave in and allowed the rest to flow down her cheeks.

She sang the last note and a hush came over the crowd. Through her blurred vision, she looked at their faces. Tears flowed from many of their eyes.

Before she could escape, Beau gripped her in a bear hug. "Well done, Bella. Well done."

"Thank you, Beau," she said softly.

He held a moment longer then released her. "Go back to Shane now."

As Bella made her way down the aisle, her heart felt too big for her chest. *Go back to Shane now.*

She smiled at him with a blush rising in her cheeks. Knowing this man had changed her. And because of him, she no longer wanted to grasp at the past.

Once settled in their pew, she lowered her head, reached up and released the clasp of William's necklace. She balled the locket in her fist and looked back into Shane's eyes.

He blinked at her, lowered his gaze to her hand.

She said nothing, simply set the necklace on the floor and kicked it gently under the pew ahead of her.

Her hand felt light, empty. Until Shane reached out and placed his palm against hers, right in the spot the necklace had occupied earlier.

A sigh lifted from deep within her. She looked into his eyes and saw the forgiveness she'd been craving ever since she'd seen his stricken face in Mattie's parlor.

With his acceptance, she'd taken her first step toward mending the wound William had inflicted on her heart. Now, she must turn to God and trust Him.

As she clung to Shane, fingers twined tightly with his, words were impossible and completely unnecessary. So they sat that way, hand in hand, for the rest of the service.

Chapter Seventeen

By the time Shane led Bella down the church steps, the early-morning breeze had built into a cold, raw wind. One sniff and he could smell the coming snow like a nasty threat. Not a good day for strolling. Thankfully, the Scott's house was a block away.

Huddled inside her wool coat, Bella smiled up at him. Her rosy, wind-chapped cheeks peeked out from beneath her hat, making her look young and healthy. Returning her smile, Shane boldly took her hand in his.

Heads bent together against the wind, they trekked along in companionable silence. Looking up, Shane glanced at the great mountains in the distance. He loved the untamed beauty of the Rockies, but today the compelling scenery held no real interest for him.

He had other, more important, thoughts on his mind.

From the moment he'd escorted Bella into church, Shane had sensed a change between them, a subtle shift toward a daring new future together. When she'd taken off the viscount's necklace, Shane had pressed his hand into hers and had accepted the truth. He was in love with Bella O'Toole.

But what would come of it?

Heart pounding like the wild wind, Shane opened the Scotts' backdoor and stepped aside so Bella could enter the mudroom first. Following closely behind her, a wave of enveloping warmth hit him as he shut the door behind them. Shrugging out of his coat, he helped Bella remove hers and then hung both garments on the wall hooks to his left.

Shane cleared his throat. "After dinner, perhaps we could talk?"

She pulled off her cap and her hair tumbled like a golden waterfall past her shoulders. "I'd like that."

There was so much gratitude, so much relief in her eyes that he realized his initial reaction to her revelations yesterday had hurt her deeply.

He pushed at his hair, started to apologize but was cut off by a delighted squeal.

"Miss Bella!" Ethan Scott launched himself in the air.

Bella swiveled just in time to catch the boy mid-flight. "Oh. Oh, my." Sounding a little breathless, she lifted the boy higher in her arms. "And how is my favorite four-year-old?"

Ethan's face spread into a brilliant smile. "Happy, now that you're here."

"I'm glad to see you, too." A shaft of sunlight streamed through the window behind her, glittering through her hair like polished gold.

Shane gulped. Looking at Bella O'Toole made his heart hurt.

Oblivious to everything except the woman holding him, Ethan patted her cheek with his palm. "Want to play checkers with me?"

Still smiling, she set the child on the ground and took his hand in hers. "I can't think of a happier way to spend the afternoon."

She looked back at Shane over her shoulder. "Would you mind?"

"I suppose I can spare you for a few minutes. You'll take care of her for me?" He winked at the boy.

Ethan puffed out his little chest. "Of course."

Tripping slightly as Ethan yanked her forward, Bella gave Shane an apologetic smile as she half trotted, half skipped behind her new friend.

At the look of pure adoration in the child's eyes, Shane felt an odd twinge of jealousy. Which made no sense. The boy was nothing more than an infatuated child. Perfectly harmless.

Ashamed of himself, Shane inhaled the smell of a happy home.

He drew in another breath. Apple pie, meat, potatoes. Shane had smelled these same scents at Charity House often enough. But he couldn't recall the welcoming scents in a single childhood memory. The aromas of his youth had been rotting fish, stale liquor, dirt and mold.

Here in Denver, Shane had found freedom from that life. But would his half sisters have a satisfying future, as well? Would they survive under the impossible restrictions of their father's will?

Yes, they would. Shane would see to it himself. Once he figured out a way around the stipulation. He had two days before Mr. Wilson returned. Unfortunately, he had yet to come up with a viable solution that would satisfy everyone involved.

Perhaps Bella had been right. He was thinking too hard, trying to figure out the solution on his own, instead of allowing God to take control.

Shane cast his glance heavenward and prayed for guidance. *Lord, You have the perfect answer. I pray You reveal it to me in the next two days.*

Molly chose that moment to skip into the mudroom.

"Hi, Dr. Shane. Miss Bella told us you were out here." She planted two tiny fists on narrow hips. "What ya doing staring up at the ceiling like that?" She craned her neck to follow his gaze. "I don't see nothing up there."

"You don't see *anything* up there," Katherine said from the doorway.

Molly pressed her lips into a grumpy line and scowled at her mother. "Do you have to correct me on Sunday, too?"

With affection in her eyes, Katherine tugged on her daughter's braid. "I'm a schoolteacher, darling. It's what I do."

"Well. In that case." Molly gave her a pointed look. "I'm going to find Papa."

"He's in his office," Katherine offered without a hint of insult in her tone.

Molly darted off in the opposite direction. Katherine caught her by the sleeve. "And while you're in there, please inform him Dr. Shane and Miss O'Toole have arrived," she said before releasing her daughter.

Molly tossed a wave over her head.

Katherine sighed. "Honestly, that girl. She's becoming more and more like her father every day. Rash, impetuous, stubborn."

"And you wouldn't have her any other way," Shane reminded her.

Katherine grinned. "No, I wouldn't." She motioned him to join her. "Come in the kitchen with me. Let's talk while I finish rolling out the biscuits."

There was something in her eyes as she spoke, a female cunning that made Shane falter in his steps. Surely he was misreading her intentions. Her request was an innocent invitation to discuss the dismal weather.

He hoped.

With a bracing swallow, Shane entered the Scotts' spacious kitchen just as Katherine rounded the large chopping block in the middle of the room.

"How's Ethan's leg healing?" he asked.

"Other than the scar, you wouldn't know he'd been hurt at all."

"No limping. No—"

"He's fine, Shane." She gave him a curious look, one he couldn't fully decipher. "The wound has completely healed, just like you said it would."

Unsure what that odd look in her eyes meant, Shane

pressed the issue. "Are you sure there's no problem with the leg?"

"None."

"Well, then. All right."

Capturing a smile between her teeth, she placed her palms in a pile of flour, grabbed a hunk of dough and began kneading the lump. "Tell me, how's your assistant fairing after the measles outbreak?"

The way Katherine said "your assistant" put Shane on his guard. Clearly, the woman was heading toward an uncomfortable topic, but not understanding her motive, Shane answered the question directly. "Miss O'Toole is handling her duties very well."

"She's been a blessing to you, then."

"Yes."

"Lovely."

Shane didn't like the smirk on Katherine's lips. Every male instinct told him to leave. Get out, now, before he fumbled into a female trap. "What are you about, Katherine? Why all the questions?"

"Just confirming my suspicion."

He narrowed his eyes. "Which is?"

"You've fallen in love with Miss O'Toole."

"No." He quickly responded. "I—"

"Oh, don't deny it. I mean, really, why wouldn't you? She's smart, beautiful and has the voice of a songbird. Clearly, she feels the same toward you. It's in the way she looks at you." Katherine pointed a finger in the air near her own eyes.

Pride, temper, a hundred other messy emotions had

him speaking his greatest fear aloud. "I think she might still be in love with another man, a man she left behind in London."

Katherine's eyes widened and her hands stilled over the dough. "Oh." She looked into his eyes a moment longer, and then shook her head. "No. That's not true. You're mistaken."

How could she be so certain? And who was she to have this conversation with him?

"I won't speak about this with you, Katherine. It's not appropriate." His tone took on a harder edge than he'd planned. But in his haste to end the conversation, he'd revealed too much, said too much. And he couldn't take back the words now that they'd been spoken aloud.

"If you won't discuss this with me, then with whom? Lest you forget, doctor, you once proposed to me."

A direct hit. A sucker punch straight at his gut. "That was a long time ago. And lest *you* forget, you turned me down."

She held his stare.

Shane turned away. Where were the others? Why had they left him alone with Katherine and her incessant questions?

"I wasn't in love with you, Shane," she added. "And you certainly weren't in love with me."

Cringing, Shane knew where she was going now. And he didn't want to dredge up ancient history. "That was a different time, Katherine, a different situation. Molly had just been in a fistfight defending your honor. You were both facing real scandal. The talk had to be stopped before Molly got hurt any more than she already had."

Katherine flicked her wrist at his feeble attempt to defend himself. "I didn't care about the talk. With my mother an infamous madam, I'd faced scandal all my life."

"My offer wasn't solely about you." Shane crossed his arms over his chest and scowled. "I wanted to spare Molly a childhood of whispers. She deserved better than that. *Every* child deserves better than that."

Sighing, Katherine grabbed a towel and wiped the dough off her palms. "Don't misunderstand me. I thought your gesture was sweet."

There had been nothing sweet about his motives at the time. He'd have done anything to prevent an innocent child from living the life he'd suffered. Agitated now, Shane tapped the toe of his shoe on the floor.

"Do you remember what else I told you that day?"

Tap. Tap, tap, tap. "Go on, Katherine, have your say and be done with it."

She shot him a triumphant smile. "I told you that one day you would fall in love and understand why I had to refuse your offer."

Spreading his feet apart, Shane lowered his arms to his sides. "All right. Let's go with your logic for a moment."

She cast a glance to the heavens. "At last."

He ignored her rude outburst. "You refused my proposal because you were in love with another man. Correct?"

Eyes wary, she inclined her head. "I don't think I like your tone."

"You were right."

That caught her unaware. "I…I was?"

"Yes." He clenched his teeth a moment, then relaxed his jaw. "And I promise you this. I will never again make an offer of marriage to a woman who is pining for another man."

He had more pride than that.

Unfortunately, Katherine seemed unimpressed with his declaration. "Oh, now I understand. Because you think there's someone else back in London, you won't pursue Miss O'Toole for yourself."

"Correct." And that should have been the end of it. Except he was conversing with a female, one who liked to talk a subject to death.

"He isn't here, is he?"

Stunned by her boldness, Shane looked at her, blinking hard. Where was she going with this new line of questioning? "No, he's not," he said carefully.

"Well, then, fight for her."

Fight for her? The outrageous idea staggered him and he took a step back.

What if Shane did what Katherine suggested and ultimately failed to win Bella's heart? But what if he failed because he didn't even try?

Heavy in thought, he walked to the window overlooking the Scotts' backyard. Eyes blind to the fierce storm brewing outside, he pondered Katherine's suggestion.

Fight for her…

Laughing loudly, Trey and Molly sauntered into the kitchen.

Shane cut off his thoughts and spun around to face the newcomers. Trey's gaze connected with Shane's and his eyes narrowed to small slits. Grimacing, he turned to his wife. "What did you do to him?"

Lifting a shoulder, she went back to kneading her dough as though they'd been talking about nothing more important than the weather. The woman had gumption, Shane would give her that.

"Katherine?" Trey urged.

"I didn't do anything to him," she murmured.

"Katherine, darling, the poor man looks poleaxed."

She jerked her chin at him. "Oh, all right, I may have pointed out an error or two in his thinking."

Trey clicked his tongue at her. "We had this discussion. You promised no meddling."

"I did no such thing."

"You didn't promise, or you didn't meddle?"

Shane's question precisely.

Grimacing, she pounded her fists into the dough but she kept her lips pressed tightly together.

Trey shook his head at his impossible wife, kissed her straight on the lips then turned back to Shane.

"Come on, my friend. I'm no authority but from that hunted look in your eyes I'd say you were a man on the verge of escape. Oh, wait." He tapped a finger against his badge. "I *am* an authority on such matters."

"Marshal Scott to the rescue," Shane muttered, only half-joking as he followed hard on the other man's heels.

* * *

Later that afternoon, Bella walked silently next to Shane as he escorted her to Hannah and Beau's home. Since the distance between the two houses was only a few short blocks, she decided to enjoy every moment of their time together.

The air was cold and pure, but the threat of heavy snow had passed with the clouds an hour ago. Smiling, she cast her gaze to the clear heavens. She'd never imagined a sky could look that blue.

Lowering her head, she eyed the mansions on her left. The thin blanket of snow on the lawns gave her a sense of homecoming. Bella O'Toole had finally arrived where she belonged.

And, wonder of wonders, there was no stage in sight.

In the last few weeks, something had changed inside her. Something remarkable. It had started with this man walking solemnly beside her and, of course, with his job offer.

She'd always thought of herself as an opera singer. Nothing more and certainly nothing less. But now, she realized how shallow her life had become. Traveling from role to role, she'd grown obsessed with her craft, and had unconsciously turned her art into her idol. She had put her career ahead of her Heavenly Father.

There is no God but one...

Bella bowed her head. *Forgive me, Lord.*

Her mistake with William had come about because she'd lost sight of her priorities. But instead of confessing and moving forward in victory, she'd allowed shame to eat away at her confidence in Christ. Removing William's locket had been her first real step toward repentance.

And now, free from the viscount at last, she could open her heart to a man who would help her become a better person.

She turned her gaze to Shane. His expression wasn't exactly closed, but it wasn't welcoming either.

He was probably thinking about his current dilemma with his father's will. Mr. Wilson would want his answer in two short days.

How had she forgotten?

"Shane, do you—"

"I was proud—" he said at the same time. Cutting himself off with a chuckle, he continued, "Go ahead, Bella."

"You first."

"All right." He stopped walking.

Bella did the same.

"I want to tell you how proud I was of you in church today."

"I—" She smiled at him. "Thank you."

He gave her a poignant smile and something fluttered in her stomach. He understood. He *knew* that the famous opera singer had been terrified of singing in front of her brother's tiny congregation. "I couldn't have done it without knowing you," she added.

"You're stronger than you think." His expression turned sad, troubled even. "You've been obedient to God in a way most women given the same situation would never have been."

She lowered her gaze to her toes. This was not an easy conversation, especially with a man who had experienced the ugly repercussions of an unholy alliance between a man and his mistress.

If there was to be any relationship with him she had to be honest now, as honest as possible. Honest enough to scare him off. "I ran away, Shane. Who's to say what I would have done had I stayed?"

"Running away, as you put it, took courage, Bella, especially given your feelings for your suitor at the time."

She saw the unspoken question in his eyes and knew her answer would set them on a new path. "I don't love him anymore."

His gaze searched her face for a long moment. Bella held his stare, unflinching under his scrutiny. She had nothing to hide from him.

"Are you sure, Bella? Completely sure?"

"Yes." She put all her feelings, all her emotions into that lone word.

"You've only been here a few months. Can love die that quickly?" There was doubt in his eyes as he spoke.

"What I felt for William wasn't love. I know that now." And what she felt for Shane, the admiration, the respect, the desire to see him happy, was so much truer, deeper and real than her feelings for Lord Crawley had ever been.

"How do you know that, Bella?"

"Because…"

He lifted a single brow, hope flickering in his gaze.

"Because." She placed her hand on his cheek and smiled. "I love you."

Chapter Eighteen

Shane's first instinct was to pull Bella into his arms and swing her round and round with pleasure. She loved him. He loved her. The rest would work itself out. Except life and love didn't always end happy.

Thus, his second instinct was to step back from her declaration.

How could she love him when her heart had yearned for another man until very recently?

His tangled emotions must have shown on his face because Bella lowered her hand from his cheek. "You don't believe me."

She looked so downtrodden, so dejected, that he wanted to deny her words. But he refused to lie. "No. I don't. But Bella, I want to."

She nodded, resignation slumping her shoulders forward. Shane almost felt the need to comfort her. But then her chin shot up and her eyes grew determined. "I'll prove myself to you."

He swallowed back a hasty response. His life had found a perfect tempo with this woman, yet he couldn't trust what they had was real. Why did his past still have such power over him? Why couldn't he forgive his mother and father, and truly live his life for himself?

He looked at Bella then, really looked at her, and tried to separate both of their pasts from the present.

Caution got the best of him. "Bella, you were in love with another man only a few days ago."

Her jaw went rigid and she swallowed hard. "I told you that wasn't love. It was a whim."

The wind kicked up, howling and snapping at them with vicious delight.

"A whim," he said through flat lips.

She opened her mouth, sighed, shook her head. "I understand why you don't believe me. And I realize words alone won't convince you. So you'll have to give me time to show you my feelings are real."

Time? She asked too much of him. How could he spend countless days and nights, working side by side with her, and not fall deeper in love with her? And when she went back to the stage, or to her viscount, or wherever her next *whim* took her, he'd be left behind. Alone. Pining.

"What happens when you return to the stage?" he asked.

She shifted her stance. "Maybe I don't want to return to the stage."

Not return to the stage? She'd been born to sing. "What is this really about, Bella?"

She scowled. "I don't know what you mean."

"Don't you?" He placed his finger under her chin and applied gentle pressure until she looked into his eyes. "People don't change this dramatically in such a short period of time. And even if they did, I heard you today. You would be wasting God's gift if you never sang again."

"How do you know I didn't find my calling today?" Her eyes lit with an inner fire, a sureness he'd never seen in her before. "How do you know I wasn't meant to sing in church, praising God, not on a stage demanding the audience's worship for myself?"

Now she sounded angry. Truly angry. But he couldn't let either of them forget she was young. Her sheltered youth hadn't prepared her for the harsher realities of the world. How could either of them be sure she knew her own mind when less than two months ago she was charging to the top of the opera world, with a viscount pursuing her for his mistress?

"You'll see, Shane, as the days pass I will remain constant."

He would see nothing of the kind. And he knew the exact way to save them both from further pain.

It's the coward's way out, a voice whispered in his head. He ignored the thought as he walked her to the front of her brother's home.

He stopped before taking the first step leading to the porch. "Your services are no longer needed at this time, Miss O'Toole."

"You're dismissing me? *Again?*" Her voice was one of pure outrage, as though no one had ever dared to disagree with her on a matter more than once, much less twice in two days.

Had she been upset by his words, contrite even, Shane might have changed his mind. Instead, he stood his ground. "As of this afternoon, you are no longer my assistant."

Her mouth hung open, then it shut with a determined snap. "We've been through this before."

"Yesterday, to be exact."

Her eyebrows slammed together. Shane could see her mind working through the conversation, coming up with and then discarding several responses. At last, a look of triumph spread across her face.

Shane braced for impact.

"Technically, you can't dismiss me because you don't pay me. I'm a volunteer."

"Not anymore."

She balled her hands into tight fists by her sides. "You are the most stubborn man I know."

"And you're the picture of flexibility." His ironic tone made her frown.

"You will regret this," she warned.

"Probably."

With a blink and a snap of her head, she wrapped her dignity around her like a cloak. "I won't go quietly."

"I'm not at all surprised."

Angry shock leapt into her face. "You need me."

If she only knew how much.

"Please don't do this to me. To us."

He hated that he was hurting her. But he couldn't relent now that he had taken this step. Maybe he needed to prove to her, as much as to himself, that she wouldn't run away from love. Maybe they *both* needed to know her love for Shane was real.

With that thought, he held himself back, folded his emotions further inside himself and fought an overwhelming urge to pull her into his arms and beg her forgiveness.

"Good day, Miss O'Toole." He turned on his heel and left her sputtering after him.

As he walked away, he feared he'd made the biggest mistake of his life. Not only had he turned his back on the woman he loved, he'd just angered a very determined female. One who would not slink away meekly.

Oddly enough, the thought made him smile.

The following morning, Bella begged a ride into town from Beau. Ever the devoted brother, he delivered her to Shane's office at precisely nine o'clock. Of course, the stubborn mule of a doctor was off making his daily visits without her.

Well, she wouldn't allow him to dismiss her so easily. Thankfully, he'd forgotten to retrieve the key he'd given her that first day of work.

She let herself into the office, stood just inside the door inhaling the scent of iodine and sulfur. A sense of rightness filled her. This was where she belonged, with Shane, working by his side.

How far they'd come since the first morning of her employ. No, *she* had come far. Shane had remained the same. Convicted in his beliefs, compassionate, a true man of integrity. On his best day, William was only half the man Shane was on his worst. She'd been dazzled by the viscount. But she loved Shane.

Of course, convincing Shane she knew the difference between the two was going to be a problem. His cruel father and selfish mother had inflicted too much damage to him when he was a boy. And now, Shane didn't believe in his fellow man, or fellow woman, as was the case with Bella.

She trudged to the table and noticed that Peter Ford's will was where Mr. Wilson had left it. By its position, she realized Shane hadn't read a single page. She ran her finger across the top edge and sighed. How was he going to find a solution when he wouldn't read the stipulation for himself?

Oh, Lord, help Shane.

He deserved an answer that would hurt no one, not even himself. Yet, according to Mr. Wilson, the will was written in such a way as to ensure Shane lived with regrets the rest of his life.

Bella flipped through the pages, not really focusing on the words. She prayed the solicitor was mistaken, he had to be mistaken.

Starting over, Bella carefully read each page. Most of the legal language confused her, but then she came to the stipulation of Shane's inheritance.

"This agreement is contingent on Shane Bartlett practicing medicine in New York City," she read aloud. "If he fails to do so, my complete estate is bequeathed to Harvard Medical School for the sole purpose of research."

There it was, in black ink on white parchment, the

stipulation that condemned Shane to a lifetime of regret and guilt. No matter what course he chose, the requirement meant Shane had to move to New York or forfeit his inheritance to his alma mater.

Anger swelled. "No. I'm missing something."

With a fast flip, Bella turned to the last page. The will was dated less than a year ago.

The beast. The nasty, unfeeling beast. Peter Ford must have known about Shane's work in Denver at the time he'd drawn up his will. The old man must have known what he was doing.

And then to leave his own daughters completely without provision? "Nasty, nasty man."

Pounding her fists against her thighs, Bella paced around the room. Surely, there was a way out of the legal restrictions set before Shane.

This agreement is contingent on Shane Bartlett practicing medicine in New York...

Bella stopped pacing and rushed back to the table. *Oh, Lord, is that it? Can it be that simple? Could Peter Ford have been that shortsighted?*

Surely a man of such vast wealth wasn't so bent on getting his own way that he'd miss something so simple.

Bella flipped through the pages frantically.

"Slow down, slow down," she whispered. "Make sure you're correct."

Reading carefully, slowly, taking meticulous care with each line, Bella found Shane's solution.

Oh, Lord, You are a good and gracious God. You really do take care of Yours. Thank You, Lord. Thank You.

She gathered the papers and stuffed them in her satchel. Shane might not believe she loved him. He might not believe she was over William. But he would hear her out this morning.

Oh, yes. Shane Bartlett was in for a little lesson when it came to Bella O'Toole's devotion to him.

And for his sake, he better listen up the first time.

Chapter Nineteen

Shane wanted to believe Bella loved him. But as his feet led him in the direction of her brother's home, he couldn't prevent his skepticism from mounting. Years of boyhood trauma had left him cynical. Thoughts of his youth had Shane's mind wandering back to his mother.

Even now, as a successful adult, his heart yearned for the woman Amanda Bartlett had never been. Her unrequited love for Peter Ford had left her bitter. And because of her resentment, she had abandoned her duties as a mother, imprisoning Shane in a world of poverty and loneliness.

He waited for his anger to rise at the memories deluging him. But all he experienced was an overwhelming sadness. How could he condemn his mother when he himself had fallen into her same trap? He was in love with a woman whose heart was still tangled with another man's.

Caught inside his troubling thoughts, Shane nearly crashed into Beau.

Beau braced his hands on Shane's shoulders. "Whoa, watch yourself."

"Sorry." With a shake of his head, Shane forced his mind back to the present. He heard laughter coming from Charity House's backyard, heard the sound of wagon wheels rolling along, the call of a bird, Beau's impatient click of his tongue. "Someone's in a rush."

"I have a lot on my mind."

Beau slapped him on the back. "I'm sure it's nothing an honest discussion between friends can't fix."

Shane cocked his head at that cryptic remark. "I'm afraid I'm not following you."

"Come have a cup of coffee with me. We need to talk." Beau punctuated his words with a measuring half smile. Shane had seen the look before, in the Charity House kitchen when he'd first asked Bella to become his assistant. Beauregard O'Toole, firmly ensconced in his role as protective big brother, wanted to discuss his sister.

And although Shane had searched out his friend for that very reason, he found himself reluctant to carry on with his mission now. "I have to check on my patients at Charity House first."

Beau was not to be put off. "They're in the middle of a baseball game. You won't be missed for a while yet."

Recognizing the hard purpose in the other man's eyes, Shane resisted the urge to rub at the sudden headache drumming behind his eyes. "I should let them know where I'll be."

"Already done. Now come, Shane." Beau gave him a look that was not becoming to a preacher. "It's past time we had ourselves a little heart-to-heart."

Shane had a quick impression of what a man felt like on his way to a firing squad. "Maybe we should go back to my office."

"We do this in my office today."

Beau took off toward his house. Shane had no other recourse but to follow. Or rather, no other recourse besides running away like a yellow-belly coward.

"We'll talk in my study," Beau suggested.

Trailing behind his friend, Shane removed his coat, all the while thinking hard. Something had spurred this meeting. And he feared he knew what. Bella. Him. Together, with *together* being the operative word.

One slim thought held his rising desperation at bay. Shane had remained above reproach in his behavior with his friend's sister. *More or less.*

As they filed into the study, Shane took in the dark paneled walls, the smooth leather chairs and the wide oak desk on top of rich-colored rugs. All that was missing was a sign that read No Girls Allowed.

Beau dropped into the chair behind his desk, and then kicked his feet on top, crossing his ankles over one another. Hands clasped behind his head, he shut his eyes and took a deep breath.

Clearly, the man was relishing this moment in his private retreat.

Unsure what Beau was about, Shane settled into one of the wingback chairs facing the other man and waited.

It didn't take long for Beau to open his eyes and settle his gaze on Shane. Although in a seemingly relaxed posture, he'd positioned himself in such a way that there could be no doubt this was not a casual get-together.

Shane sent up a fervent prayer for guidance. "What's on your mind, Beau?"

"Actually." Beau dropped his feet to the floor and leaned on his desk, pressing his weight on his forearms. "That's what I'd like to know."

Shane considered himself an intelligent man, but no matter how he mulled over Beau's words, he didn't understand the question. Was the man talking in some convoluted preacher code? Had Shane missed a portion of the conversation? "Speak clearly."

Beau's gold eyes glittered as he studied Shane in that thorough, patient way that had sinners spilling their guts.

"How's this for clear speaking," Beau said. "What's on your mind when it comes to my little sister?"

Shane reared back in his chair. "That was certainly direct."

"Are your intentions honorable?"

Shane fought a hard battle to keep his voice steady. "I have no intentions, honorable or otherwise." None he cared to share with her big brother, at least.

"Why not?"

"Pardon me?"

Beau settled back into his chair with a grin lifting the corners of his lips. "Why aren't you pursuing my sister?"

Shane drew in a hard breath. "Bella is my assistant. It would be inappropriate to *pursue her,* as you put it."

Could he sound any more pompous?

"Inappropriate. Hmm." Beau gave him a look just short of insulting. "But holding hands in church is altogether suitable?"

Shane's heart pounded with regret. He should have known that particular detail would come out at some point, but he'd been too stupid to prepare a defense.

"It was innocent enough." Shane stabbed a glance at the door. Maybe he could leave before this got ugly.

"Have you kissed her yet?"

Too late.

But...

Now wait...

If Shane wasn't mistaken, Beau's eyes danced with...delight?

"What is wrong with you?" Shane ground out. "You're Bella's brother. Aren't you supposed to be upset I've been chasing after your sister when I promised to protect her while in my care? Yet all along I've been thinking about...wanting to...that is..."

Shane gripped the arms of the chair and let his words trail off. His chest tightened at what he'd nearly revealed.

Despite Shane's telling admission, Beau continued calmly blinking at him, his gaze patient and unwavering as though he had all the time in the world to wait for Shane to collect his thoughts and continue.

Shane had nothing more to say.

At last, Beau broke the silence. "I just have one more question."

"Fair enough."

"Do you love her?"

Why lie now? Why turn this farce of a meeting into something uglier than it had already become? "Yes."

Beau muttered something under his breath about godsends and blessings, then added a little louder, "Then I return to my earlier question. Why aren't you pursuing her?"

"It's not that simple."

"Why not?"

"We... I... It... It just isn't." Shane shut his mouth. He was blathering like an idiot. But what was he supposed to say? He couldn't disclose the reasons for his reluctance to begin a personal relationship with Bella. To do so, he would have to reveal her liaison with the viscount. That wasn't Shane's secret to tell.

"She calls you Shane, you call her Bella. You hold hands in church. The way I see it, it's very simple." Beau said. "All I ask is that you court her properly."

Shane looked away from Beau's well-meaning advice. *Court her properly. Fight for her.* Bottom line, if Shane had any chance of happiness he had to stop waffling where Bella was concerned. He had to act. He had to—

The door burst open and in spilled the very subject of his thoughts. "Shane. I've been looking for you everywhere. There's no residency clause, no time restrictions. Don't you see? That's your answer. It's... Oh!" Her voice trailed off and she simply looked from one man to the other.

Shane rose and stared at Bella. He knew what he had to do. No more doubt. No more allowing the past to rule his actions. It was time he made some concrete decisions. No. It was time he did some proper courting.

Bella looked from one man to the other and then repeated the process two more times. They were two big, beautiful males. And the masculine backdrop of Beau's office only added to the strong impression they made as they stared at her.

The fact that these men neither realized nor cared how handsome they were made them all the more appealing. Without an ounce of vanity, they were a little too large, a little too confident and utterly terrifying.

Gathering her courage, her eyes connected with Shane's. "I'll come back later," she said.

"No." Beau rose from his chair. "I was just leaving. Shane has something he wants to say to you." He looked pointedly at Shane. "Isn't that right?"

Shane nodded.

Bella sighed. Obviously, something of monumental importance had been said about her.

More than a little agitated at the notion of her brother discussing her with Shane, she stepped to one side to make a path for Beau's exit.

But instead of looking at her brother as he approached, she kept her eyes on Shane. The intensity of his gaze reminded her of the first time they'd met when Ethan had cut his leg. Even then, before she'd known him, she'd sensed he was a man who made things better for those around him. She hadn't known he would change her life so dramatically.

Good thing she liked drama.

Through loving him, Bella had learned to think of another. To worry for another's well-being and happiness above her own.

Bella had found her life's partner in Shane. It was time he quit fighting her and accepted that fact.

Before exiting the room, Beau stopped beside her and squeezed her hand. "Be tough, Bella. Relentless, as you are with everything that truly matters to you."

As she stared into her brother's eyes she saw the truth there. He understood. Shane had revealed enough for Beau to know the situation. And now, he was telling her to battle for the man she loved.

And so she would.

Beau closed the door behind him with a soft click. For a long moment, Bella and Shane didn't move, didn't breathe. They were caught in some sort of odd moment in time, as if they were locked inside a photograph.

At last, Shane broke eye contact and looked at the satchel she carried. He lifted a questioning brow.

"I found your solution," she said.

"Yes?"

"I'll show you."

Glad for the distraction, she slid past him, pulling the papers out of the case as she walked. With a thump, she set Peter Ford's will on top of Beau's desk and gestured Shane forward. "Page six. Read the tenth line."

He slowly joined her, trepidation sparkling in his eyes.

"Trust me, Shane." They both knew she spoke of more than his father's will.

His steps faltered. Then he smiled. Really smiled. "Let's see what you found."

She took a shaky breath and turned the pages for him.

He bent his head over the will. She waited as his gaze flew down the page. And then his eyes stopped moving.

"Read it out loud," she suggested.

Glancing up, he cocked his head at her then lowered his gaze again. "This agreement is contingent on Shane Bartlett practicing medicine in New York City."

Impatience had her tapping her foot on the hardwood floor. "Well?"

He looked at her, looked back at the will. "I don't—"

"There's no residency clause. There's nothing specifically requiring you to live in New York City."

"Bella, darling, I can't practice medicine if I'm not in the city."

He'd called her darling. Oh, the dear, dear man.

"You could live here. Travel there four times a year."

He stood rigidly, with the unforgiving posture of a man who refused to yield. "Patients require day-to-day care."

"Then hire partners, doctors who will be there for the day-to-day care. With your father's money you could afford to hire several nurses, as well."

Shane swallowed a few times and she realized he didn't know how to respond.

"It's not a perfect solution, but it could work."

"We'll have to check the legalities," he said slowly. "And, of course, we'd have to find the right doctors. But if you're correct, I could have a clinic both here *and* in New York."

Her eyes lit up. "Oh, Shane. That's precisely what I was thinking."

His gaze locked on a point above her head. "Women like my mother would have decent medical care here and in my old neighborhood." A slow grin spread across his face. "My father would hate that."

"And best of all, you could afford to care for your sisters, as well."

"Thanks be to God."

Bella smiled. "The Lord has blessed you, Shane. Just like I knew He would."

Shoving the papers slightly away from him, Shane pierced Bella with one of his most intense looks to date. "Bella O'Toole, whether you're right or not, the real blessing in my eyes is that you cared enough to look for an answer."

She gave him a shaky smile, realizing no person in his life had cared enough for Shane. Not his mother and certainly not his father. "Of course I looked. I love you, Shane."

Blinking, he pulled her into his arms and held her close. "I love you, too," he whispered into her hair.

She flung her wrists around his neck and clung to him. "It's about time you admitted it."

His hold tightened. "Tell me you love me, Bella. I want to hear you say it again."

"I love you, Shane. With all my heart."

She felt him relax against her. Bella's pulse slowed to a lovely cadence, beating in perfect time with Shane's. *This* was where she belonged. *Oh, thank You, Lord.*

Slowly, deliberately, he released her. "We have a lot to talk about. Your past and mine will always be between us if we don't settle our differences now."

She tugged her bottom lip between her teeth and allowed herself a moment of hope. "I found a passage in Scripture that I think applies. It's from Luke, in the story about the woman who comes to wash Jesus's feet."

"One who is forgiven little loves little," he quoted from memory.

"Yes. And it goes without saying, a person who is forgiven a lot, loves a lot." She smiled. "You know, Shane, I have *a lot* of love to give."

"As do I."

They laughed. He took her hand in his, brought it to his lips. A wave of affection washed over her. She had found the man of her dreams. But the moment his mouth brushed her knuckles, a soft knock came at the door.

"Bella?" Hannah's lilting voice seeped into the room. "Are you in there?"

Shane released Bella's hand. "We'll talk later," he said.

Bella gripped his arm, a wave of desperation filled her. "Tonight? After we've finished seeing patients?"

"Of course." He smiled at her. "After *we* finish seeing patients."

"Does that mean you're hiring me back?"

He ducked his head. "I should have never fired you."

"I knew you'd see things my way."

"What can I say?" He winked. "I'm a reasonable man."

"Oh. I like reasonable men."

A grin flashed across his lips. "Come in, Hannah,"

Shane called out. "Before Bella has me promising her the moon and the stars and a rainbow or two."

Hannah popped her head through a small slit. Her gaze slid to Shane in silent apology. "Bella has a visitor."

At the softly spoken words, a sense of foreboding filled Bella. The same feeling must have passed through Shane, because he stiffened at Hannah's announcement.

Bella reached to Shane for support. "Who…who is it?"

In answer, Hannah handed her a small piece of paper with engraved lettering on it. "He gave me his card."

Reading the name, Bella's knees buckled. Shane reached out to steady her.

Tucked in the safety of his arms, she let the card flutter from her fingers. "It's William," she whispered. "He's come for me."

Chapter Twenty

Powerless to stop her life from spiraling out of control, Bella clung to Shane as he helped her catch her balance. When he set her away from him and left nothing but lifeless air between them, she thought, *Surely, this can't be real.* William couldn't be here. Not in her brother's home.

But he was.

And the look of defeat that flashed in Shane's eyes added to the reality of this horrible moment.

He started for the door.

Her hand shot out and stopped his progress. "Shane, no, don't go." *Help me, Lord. Help me to convince him to stay with me.* "I don't want this. I don't want him."

He dropped his head, took a deep breath and then lifted his flat gaze to hers. His eyes were so cold. So emotionless. But she knew he hurt. She could feel his pain in her own heart.

Oh, Shane.

"You should hear what he has to say. He's traveled a long distance for you."

"I didn't ask him to come."

"You did. By running away and ignoring his letters, you forced his hand." He cupped her cheek, his touch light and forgiving and completely at odds with the dark look in his eyes. "You have to finish what you started, Bella. You'll never know how you truly feel if you don't."

She ordered her voice to remain even, but her growing panic made her words come out shrill. "I don't need to talk to him to know how I feel."

Sympathy flashed in his gaze. "Nevertheless, you should take this opportunity to alleviate any doubt."

He was so calm, so in control. The flare of resentment surprised her and her reflex was to turn on him, but she shook it off. Shane hadn't done anything wrong. "Please. Don't leave me alone with William."

"Are you afraid of him?" Shane's eyes hardened with the look of a man protecting a woman he loved. "Will he hurt you?"

His concern cut through her anxiety. She wanted to reach up and cup his face. She wanted to kiss him and beg him to believe it was him that she loved. "No. Of course not. I—" She cut her own words off. How could she explain her real fear? How could she tell him she was terrified he might never come back once he walked out that door? "Shane, I—"

William's booming voice cut her off. "I will wait no longer. Bella? Bella!" He knocked hard on the door. "Are you in there?"

At the sound of the familiar voice, her stomach dipped and she looked frantically for an exit. There was only one door.

And Shane stepped toward it, away from her. "You must face your past, Bella. And you must do it alone."

"Shane, please."

Shaking his head, he took another step away from her. "She's in here," he called out.

The next second, William burst into the room.

Bella's pulse drummed in her ears as Shane melted into the shadows and William took another step forward.

Her first thought was that the viscount looked as handsome as ever, still tall and lean, with sharp, angular features and perfectly tailored clothing. But inside his expensive attire, William looked lost in his own image, like an actor playing an overrehearsed role.

Was this the man she'd nearly sacrificed her soul for?

As his gaze hunted for Bella, Bella's gaze strayed to Shane. He hadn't left the room yet. And although his features were curtained by the shadows, she knew he was standing ready to protect her if William crossed a line.

So caught up in staring at Shane, she nearly missed the moment when William's gaze found her.

With an exaggerated sweep of his hand he removed his hat and bowed to her. The gesture was so formal, so over the top, she wondered if it wasn't a bit calculated.

"Bella, my darling. I have found you at last."

An idle smile drifted along his lips and he reached out his hand in silent summons.

Tossing her head back, Bella refused his call. And

again, she wondered what had attracted her to the viscount. Only months before she'd been desperate for William's love. Now, she felt nothing.

"I'll leave you two alone," Shane said into the silence.

Bella reached to him. "No, stay. Please."

He must have sensed her panic because his gaze softened and he gave her the look he used when his patients thought he might abandon them during a procedure. "I'll be right outside if you need me."

William straightened, his eyes fixed on a spot over Shane's shoulder as though Shane didn't warrant his full attention. "No need to fuss over her, my good man. Bella will be leaving with me shortly."

A ruthless look crossed Shane's face. "Bella will make that decision."

Before William could respond, Shane exited the room and shut the door behind him with a hard snap.

After months of separation, she was alone with William again. Her stomach rolled over itself in trepidation, but she kept her gaze steady. William held no more power over her. The relief that came with the thought nearly buckled her knees. She wanted to shout at him to leave at once. It was over between them, finished. But she restrained herself. A moment like this required a certain amount of dignity.

Unaware of her thoughts, William bowed over her hand and touched his lips to her knuckles. "You win, my dear." Tenderness and appreciation mingled in his gaze, but she knew better than to believe in him. He was only doing what he felt he needed to do in order to accomplish his goal.

She slipped her hand free. "What have I won, William?"

"Why, my dear, isn't it obvious?" He gave her the smile she once thought so charming but now appeared a little wicked. "You have won me."

"You?" Bella couldn't quite believe the arrogance of the man and a wave of impatience whipped through her. "What exactly do you mean by that?"

"I am a free man." Seconds ticked by before he added, "My wife is dead."

At the cold tone of his voice, a shiver iced over her skin. His wife was dead? Did he not miss the woman at all? "I am sorry for your loss."

He waved a dismissive hand. "She was always sickly. Her passing was a blessing in the end."

She thought she saw a flicker of something dark in his eyes, but then he smiled, putting the suave viscount back in place. Who was this man, really? Had she ever known him?

"I want you to come home with me, Bella. Back to London where you belong."

Where she belonged? Bella caught her rising gasp between her teeth and stared at him with a steady look. She had once craved to hear him say those exact words. But home was Denver now, not London. Home was with Shane, wherever that took them. "I can't go to London with you. I want more than the stage has to offer."

The satisfaction in his eyes put her on guard. "Then we are in agreement. Whatever you want, Bella, I will provide it for you." He ran his blue eyes over her in lazy thoroughness. "I want you with me and I am willing to pay for the privilege."

Unlike the last time he'd made his proposition, his words left her cold with rage. *This time around,* she heard what he wasn't saying as much as what he said.

"Go on, William." She clasped her hands calmly together. "Tell me what you're offering. You've come this far, you might as well expand on the details."

"I will give you the security you crave."

Holding firm, Bella waited for the rest.

Nothing more came.

"Is that all you're offering?" she asked.

His facade slipped, just a bit, making him look young and spoiled. *"Is that all?"* he repeated in an offended tone. "You will have carte blanche for the rest of your life."

She tilted her head, planted her hands on her hips. He looked like a child who was being denied a pretty toy that had caught his fancy. "You mean carte blanche as your mistress."

"As the love of my life."

His haughty attitude made her take a step back, but still, she persisted. She would force him to say what was on his mind, no matter how ugly the truth. "And if you tire of me?"

"You will be taken care of no matter what happens between us in the future."

Her knees wobbled again, but she locked them into place as understanding emerged. "You mean financially, of course."

"Of course. My solicitor has drawn up the contract."

He grabbed her wrist and placed her hand to his heart. "Bella, Bella, can you not feel my heart pounding with love for you? Can you not believe I mean to take care of you for the rest of your life?"

She calmly pulled her hand free. "Am I to understand you are offering me security, but not in the form of marriage?"

Lifting his chin, he clasped his hands behind his back and drew in a long breath. "I can not marry an opera singer. It is simply not done. I have two sons, both with titles in their own right. I must take a wife of good family. But my heart will always belong to you, my love. I will simply find a woman to marry who understands this."

Bella's hand clutched at her throat. Her *bare* throat where she no longer wore William's condemning locket. She was free of him now, free of his filthy intentions. She would *not* feel shame over his sinful propositions any longer.

Before she could tell William exactly what she thought of him and his offer, Shane jerked open the door.

Beau shot in ahead of him, but Shane caught him by the sleeve and yanked him back. "This is my fight."

Her brother looked angry. Truly angry. But not as angry as Shane. Clearly, the men in her life were not going to allow anyone to hurt her.

"Fine, I will leave the matter in your hands," Beau growled. "But you better end this now. Today."

Shane's lips twisted in a sneer. "Count on it."

Bella had one second to take in her brother's answering glower before he slammed out of the room.

"Shane?"

"I'm sorry, Bella, but I won't allow history to repeat itself." His voice came out low and steadfast.

She almost missed his meaning, but then she understood. He loved her enough to ensure she didn't live his mother's life, even if that meant forcing William's hand. Who would have thought the caring doctor could be such a warrior at heart? "Oh, Shane, no, I don't need you to fight this battle for me. I have made up my—"

He cut off the rest of her words with a hard shake of his head. Like a knight guarding his lady-in-waiting, he set her gently behind him and then turned to glare at William. "Bella deserves nothing less than marriage. Offer it, or get out."

A range of emotions crossed the viscount's face, but the eyes that finally locked on Shane were sharp and measuring. "Who are you to demand this of me?"

Shane ignored the question. "You will find no woman better than Isabella O'Toole. She is kind, compassionate. Smart."

Bella cleared her throat. "Shane, you don't have to do this."

Shane patted her hand, and then shrugged away from her. "Yes, I do."

"I asked for your name," William demanded again. "Who dares to speak to me in this impudent manner?"

Their eyes locked and held.

"I am Shane Bartlett. Bella has been serving as my nurse these last few months."

"A nurse?"

Shane held up a hand at William's shocked declaration and took the opportunity to continue his litany of Bella's merits. "I have had the pleasure of working with Miss O'Toole in the sickroom. She's courageous, full of gentleness and joy and…" On and on and on he went.

Even Bella was losing track of all her fine qualities. And she wasn't one to sniff at a compliment. But with each new trait Shane presented on her behalf, William's face grew redder with outrage. If there had been a shred of doubt before, Bella no longer had to guess which man truly loved her.

And which man she loved in return.

Shane might be embellishing a bit—*a lot*—but she also realized he spoke from his heart. While William could only stare at him in growing disgust, a subtle air of disapproval floating out of his stance.

At last…finally…Shane wound down, ending with, "And, of course, she's beautiful."

"Is that all?" William asked, his tone droll.

"For a start."

"And if I don't propose marriage to this virtuous creature of perfection?" he challenged.

"I'll happily make Bella an offer myself."

"No. No. Can't have that." But William's face paled as he gazed at Bella. No longer the confident nobleman full of demands and bluster, he looked uneasy, a little ill and his breath came out in quick, hard bursts. "You have convinced me of what I must do."

Bella had never been more insulted in her life.

Shane, on the other hand, looked oddly triumphant.

What? He was going to hand her over to William, just like that? Without a fight?

"Carry on." Shane wound his wrist in the air. "But make it quick, I have patients waiting."

William swallowed, his face looking green along the edges. "I'm getting to it."

Now Bella was *truly* insulted.

Seeming in no hurry to get to his "patients," Shane crossed his arms over his chest and hitched his hip against Beau's desk. He looked a little too pleased with himself, as though he was enjoying William's discomfort. "Get on with it, *my good man.*"

"One can't rush an important matter such as this."

"It's four little words," Shane scoffed. "Can't be that hard to say. *Will you marry me?* See, I just said them myself."

William glared.

Shane grinned.

Bella sighed.

"Uh, gentlemen, I'm in the room," she reminded them. "Is anybody going to consult *me* on the matter?"

William continued scowling at Shane. Shane continued grinning in return.

And neither acknowledged Bella's question.

"Go on," Shane goaded. "Four little words and you win the girl for a lifetime."

William swallowed. Hard.

Shane's smile widened.

"Honestly." Bella interrupted the two. "I can make this simple for us all. I don't want to marry William."

They both ignored her and continued their ridiculous battle of wills.

As William's discomfort grew, Shane's confidence did the same. Bella suspected Shane was having a bit too much fun at the other man's expense. Clearly, William didn't want to marry Bella any more than she wanted to marry him. But the lofty viscount was too proud to admit that rather large detail in front of Shane.

She would have never suspected William to be so easily manipulated. Again, she wondered if she'd ever known the man.

Just when she thought the viscount would give up his pride and admit his true feelings, William surprised her. After muttering a rather nasty oath at Shane, he marched to Bella. With a final grumble under his breath, he snatched up her hand. "Bella, darling, will you marry me?" He spoke through gritted teeth.

Before answering, she drew her hand out of William's grip. Free of the contact, she actually felt her heart settle. "No."

"No?"

"I don't want marriage."

The look of relief on his face should have been humiliating, but his next words left her too cold for any emotion at all. "But you will consider—"

"Absolutely not." She and Shane said at the same time.

William looked at her then Shane scowled. "What's Bella to you, anyway?"

Shane stared at her for a long, agonizing moment.

The intensity in his gaze took her breath away. "I love her. She is everything to me, second only to God."

The man had to work on his timing, but Bella could forgive the minor transgression. Shane had declared his love in front of William, who happened to be sputtering with indignation.

Bella sighed. The sooner she ushered the viscount out of the room, the better. He didn't belong in her world now, and she didn't belong in his. He'd know that if he'd give up a portion of his pride. "William, I appreciate that you traveled this far to find me. But I choose to stay here, with Shane."

William cocked his head, a frown marring his brow. "You're staying here? With *him?* You're not even returning to the stage?"

"God has called me to a different life, one with a higher purpose."

He looked at her as though she'd grown two heads. "As what, a nurse? You'd give up the stage to care for *sick* people?"

And then she knew the truth. William had never loved her. He had merely loved the idea of her. But he hadn't known her, and he certainly wouldn't recognize the woman she'd become. A woman of faith, who would spend her life praising God with her voice and honoring Him with her hands.

She didn't have to defend her decisions, not to this man. She doubted he would understand if she tried. *Has God not made foolish the wisdom of the world?*

"I'm happy here, William. This is where I belong."

She glanced at Shane. He smiled at her with encouragement. She wanted to rush into his arms, but he'd been right all along. She had to finish what she'd started back in London.

Head high, she focused once more on William. "Go home to your sons, Lord Crawley. Find a wife for yourself, one who will be a good mother, as well. I pray she's a woman who will make you forget you ever wanted a mistress."

He looked at her as though he was a man who couldn't run fast enough in the opposite direction. "So, this is it, then? The end?"

"Goodbye, William."

She held very still as William muttered a foul word, spun on his heel and left the room without so much as a farewell thrown her way. She felt a little empty as she stared at his retreating back, as though her parting with him had been anticlimactic, nothing but a boring ending to a mediocre play.

"Shane, I have a confession to make," she said as she continued staring at the space William had recently occupied.

"Yes?"

She turned to face him, let her love shine boldly in her eyes. "I wasn't completely forthright when I said I didn't want marriage."

His gaze turned inscrutable. "No?"

"Oh, I want marriage. As a matter of fact, I *deserve* marriage."

"Yes." He smiled. "Yes, you do."

She took his hand, pressed a kiss in his palm. "But I won't settle for just any man who comes along."

"That would be a disaster."

"Precisely. I have decided I want to share my life with a man willing to sacrifice his own happiness in place of mine, a man who thinks I'm kind, compassionate, smart and all the other things you said in my defense."

"I love you, Bella."

"I love you, Shane."

She lowered to her knees. "I have four little words for you," she said with a smile. "Will you marry me?"

Frowning, he knelt beside her. "Despite my unusual upbringing, I'm a traditional man, my dear. I'm supposed to ask the question."

"Then ask it, my love."

He cupped her face between his hands and kissed her on the lips. "Will you marry me, Bella O'Toole?" He kissed her again. "Will you be my wife?" He kissed her a third time. "And my partner in serving God?"

"I have just one word to say in response."

A muscle shifted in his jaw. "Is that one word *yes?*"

She gave him a firm nod. *"Yes."*

Epilogue

June 15, 1887, New York City, the Bowery,
lower Manhattan

The day dawned clear and hot, magnifying the foul stench of unwashed bodies, rotting fish and stale whiskey. Bella wrinkled her nose as she walked alongside her husband. It wasn't what she would call the perfect fragrance to accompany a ribbon-cutting ceremony, but nothing could dampen her spirits now that this monumental day had arrived.

In a few moments, Shane would officially open the doors of the Bowery Medical Clinic to the general public. The small hospital was an exact replica of the one they'd launched six months ago in Denver, all the way down to the scrolled verse above the front door: *for we walk by faith, not by sight.*

God had provided far more than any of them could

have accomplished on their own. And it seemed the more they gave, the more they received back in joy.

They were truly blessed.

Waddling alongside Shane, Bella felt like an over-dressed, overstuffed cow. According to Hannah, seven months of pregnancy tended to do that to a woman. At least the morning sickness was gone. And yet, as Bella looked around her husband's childhood streets, bile rose in her throat.

The dark side of life was presented without any attempt to tone down the disreputable image. No decent man or woman would walk these streets at night. Even at this early hour, many of the concert halls and Dime Museums flourished with customers. Vulgar songs accompanied by wretched music spilled into the streets. The lodgings interspersed between the shady businesses were filthy beyond compare. Shane called the falling-down tenements "resorts for thieves." He would know.

The elder of Shane's two sisters, Drusilla, a pretty, blonde, round-faced sixteen-year-old spoke Bella's thoughts aloud. "Oh, Shane, how did you ever survive this place?"

Affection glittered in his eyes as Shane looped an arm over the girl's shoulder. "Simple. God protected me, my dear."

Drusilla grinned at him, sisterly adoration apparent in her eyes. "Well, I'm glad for that."

Not to be outdone, Elizabeth, the gregarious twelve-year-old and miniature version of her older brother, snatched at his other arm. "And now you've returned a hero."

He lifted a single eyebrow. "I wouldn't go that far."

"I would." She looked around her with keen interest, and a little sauciness kicked in her voice. "I think it's amazing you grew up here, no rules, no restrictions, no—"

"Food, at times," Shane reminded her.

"Of course." Elizabeth's eyes grew serious and she lowered her head. "I forgot that part."

Shane pulled her close and hugged her against him. "It's ancient history. And if I can help some of the children who live here now, well, maybe it was for the best. How would I know how to alleviate their suffering, if I hadn't experienced it myself?"

Blinking rapidly, she lifted her eyes to his. "I'm going to be a doctor just like you."

"I think that's a wonderful idea," Bella announced before Shane could offer his opinion on the matter.

Elizabeth turned her head. "You do?"

"I think you can do anything you set your mind to."

Elizabeth beamed. Emotion squeezed at Bella's heart. She loved this child dearly, just as she loved Drusilla. But most of all, she loved watching Shane interact with his sisters. Her handsome, serious-minded husband was more relaxed and definitely more affectionate because of his time spent with the girls. Yet another blessing to come from the ashes of Peter Ford's untimely death.

As soon as the legalities had been settled, Shane had sent for the girls. Thankfully, Drusilla and Elizabeth had grown to adore Shane in a very short amount of time. And Bella had won them over, as well. In truth, the girls had been desperate for real parents and now the four of them made a happy, albeit unusual, family.

Slowing her pace, Bella looked at Shane over the girls' heads. He winked at her. His code for *I love you*.

She blew him a kiss as they rounded the final corner of their destination. She froze midstep and gasped at the sight before her. Hundreds of people stood in line along the three blocks leading to 35 Bowery. "Oh, Shane, there's so many of them."

He blew out a long breath and studied the queue that snaked past brothels, beer gardens and flophouses.

"We'll do what we can," he said, looking more than a little stunned himself. "God will provide the rest."

"But it'll take a miracle," Drusilla cried in a shaky voice.

"God's specialty is miracles," Shane said with far more conviction this time. "Remember the story of the two fish and five loaves? If the Lord can feed the multitudes, He can certainly help us with this."

Drusilla slowly nodded. "I…suppose."

Taking a fortifying breath of air, Shane gripped Bella's hand and started forward. "By the grace of God we go."

Nodding, Bella took Drusilla's hand and Drusilla took Elizabeth's. As a unified family of four, they pushed their way through the throng.

Mr. Wilson and the young doctor Shane had recently hired stood behind a wide red ribbon that had been roped between two large columns in front of the clinic.

"I think it's wonderful you're using Father's money to open this hospital," Elizabeth said as they continued marching forward.

Bella couldn't agree more. Peter Ford's money was now funding medical care for the impoverished, including women much like the one he'd helped destroy. Had there been decent facilities sixteen years ago, perhaps Amanda Bartlett might still be alive.

It was a sad thought.

But this was not a day for sorrow. This was a day for joy. And celebration.

Much like he'd done in Denver, Shane escorted their group up the front steps of the clinic. Smiling, he lifted the thick ribbon high enough for them to pass under it.

After giving a short speech, he handed Bella a pair of scissors, then wrapped his hands around hers. Together, they cut the ribbon.

A loud cheer lifted from the crowd.

Turning slightly, Shane returned the scissors to Mr. Wilson. "My wife, Dr. Marsalis and I will begin seeing patients in a few moments. In the meantime, will you take my sisters home?"

The solicitor nodded. "It would be my pleasure."

Both girls jammed their fists on their hips and placed stubborn, immovable expressions on their faces.

"I want to stay," Drusilla announced.

"Me, too," Elizabeth added.

Shane shook his head at them. "Perhaps tomorrow. Today will be too chaotic."

"Bella gets to stay," Elizabeth argued.

"*Bella* has done this before." Shane's lips flattened. "I won't continue arguing with you. My decision is final." His tone brooked no argument.

Knowing when to accept defeat, the girls relented.

Among hugs and grumblings and more hugs, Bella and Shane finally sent them on their way.

Before entering the building, Shane pulled Bella aside. "Thank you, my dear, thank you for being the best wife a man could hope to have." His ocean-blue eyes shone with emotion. "You are the love of my life."

A fresh spurt of joy tickled her throat. "Shane, I'm so proud of you. I love you so much."

Pulling her close, he ran his gaze down the long line of patients. "I thought I'd escaped this neighborhood. But God had a bigger plan in mind."

"You've come full circle, my love."

He kissed her on the nose and then set her far enough away to glance at her belly. Concern marred his features. "Are you sure you're up to this today?"

"Nothing could keep me away."

A smile lifted the corner of his lips. "I'm glad. I need you by my side, Bella. As my helper, my wife and my greatest love on earth."

She lifted to her toes and touched her lips to his. "Good thing I'm not going anywhere."

"A very good thing."

They laughed together.

"Hey," shouted a man from at least a half block away. "You gonna open them doors or not?"

Shane's gaze traveled down to the man speaking, then cut back to Bella. "Let's get to work, shall we?"

His words were the same ones he'd used when Ethan Scott had hurt his leg that first day she'd arrived in Denver. This time, however, Shane was asking Bella to assist him the rest of their lives.

Lord, thank You for giving me the courage to love this man, and to do the work You've planned for us.

She boldly held her husband's gaze and allowed a driving sense of purpose to shine in her eyes. "I'm at your disposal, Dr. Shane."

He kissed her on the lips. "A man never tires of hearing that from his wife."

This time, she kissed him. "Indeed."

Arm in arm, they stepped to the front of the line and ushered the first patient inside.

* * * * *

Dear Reader,

Thank you for spending time with me at Charity House. I consider it a great privilege to share Shane and Bella's story with you.

If this is your first book with me, welcome! If you've come along for the ride before then you've probably discovered something about me as a writer. I have a heart for imperfect, flawed characters who struggle with all sorts of misconceptions about themselves. I figure I love these types of characters because I'm as human as they come, with my own share of failings. In fact, I'll let you in on a little secret about writers. Most of us don't write what we know, we write who we are. Sometimes this shows up in small ways, like a silly quirk or a favorite food or a unique talent. Other times the similarities are glaring. This particular story would be one of those "other times" in my case.

If I had to pick one of my heroines that most reflects who I am at the core it would be Bella. Not in relation to her singing talent (I can't carry a tune in a bucket), but in regards to how she allows a past mistake to define her future. I suspect Bella and I are not alone in this particular misconception. We are, after all, women. Thankfully, we also have a loving God who offers His grace on a daily basis, often minute by minute.

Have you discovered this reality in your own life? Whether this is the first time you've thought about God's grace or the thousandth, I would love to hear your story. You can contact me at www.reneeryan.com or catch me on one of those popular social networking sites found on the World Wide Web.

In the meantime, happy living, happy reading, happy days ahead!

Blessings,

Renee Ryan

QUESTIONS FOR DISCUSSION

1. In the opening scene, Bella is confronted with a shocking proposition that makes her realize how far she's strayed from God. What is this proposition? Who presents it to her? Why is she tempted, while at the same time heartbroken beyond imagining? Why do you think she didn't see this coming? Have you ever found yourself in a situation that caught you off guard like that?

2. What crisis situation led Shane to the point of desperation in the opening of chapter one? Why is he unable to find the right person for the available position? Have you ever found yourself in a similar situation, where you knew what you were doing was right despite what the world claimed?

3. Why do you think Bella accepts Shane's offer, despite her complete lack of qualification? Do you think she's motivated by selfish desires or a genuine wish to serve the Lord? Have you ever found yourself volunteering for a position for the wrong reasons? What was the result?

4. What do you think keeps Bella from accepting Hannah as a confidant? Have you ever had a situation where you were convinced nobody could relate? If so, why did you think that?

5. Why do you think Bella feels comfortable opening up to Mattie, of all people? Why do you think Bella is drawn to the "girls" in Mattie's house? Do you think God can use our past mistakes in His service? Why or why not?

6. What drives Shane to administer medical care to "undesirables" and those least accepted in the world? Do you think his service is noble or selfishly motivated? Why or why not?

7. Bella has to learn the difference between sins of the heart versus sins of the flesh. Do you think sins of the heart are easier to overcome than sins of the flesh? Why or why not? Which of the two are easier to hide?

8. What shocking information does the New York lawyer, Mr. Wilson, bring Shane? How does Shane react to the impossible terms? What solution does Bella come up with? Have you ever been in a situation that seemed impossible but ultimately worked out for the best? What was it?

9. What is Bella's terrible secret? What happens as she continues to keep it to herself? Have you ever kept something about your past hidden, only to have it come out in some unexpected way? What happened?

10. When Shane discovers Bella's secret he doubts her feelings for him are sincere. What happened in his past to make him skeptical of her declaration of love? Have you ever found it hard to believe someone's sincerity? Why or why not?

11. Bella has a surprise visitor at the end of the book. Who is it? How does she respond? What happens when she sees both William and Shane in the same room together?

12. What sacrifice does Shane make in regards to Bella? Do you think that was a noble decision on his part? How does Bella react? Does it bring about their happy ending? How?

Here's a sneak preview of
THE RANCHER'S PROMISE
by Jillian Hart
Available in June 2010 from Love Inspired

"So, are you back to stay?" Justin's deep voice hid any shades of emotion. Was he fishing for information or was he finally about to say "I told you so"?

"I'll probably go back to teaching in Dallas, but things could change. I'll just have to wait and see." The things in life she used to think were so important no longer mattered. Standing on her own two feet, building a life for herself, healing her wounds—that did.

"And this man you married?" he asked. "Did he leave you or did you leave him?"

"He threw me out." She waited for Justin's reaction. Surely a man with that severe a frown on his face was about to take delight in the irony. She'd turned down Justin's love, and her husband of five years had thrown away hers. If she were Justin, she would want her off his land.

"You were nothing but honest with me back then." He leaned against the railing, the wind raking his dark hair, and a different emotion passed across his hard countenance. "I was the one who never listened. I loved you so much, I don't think I could hear anything but what I wanted."

"I loved you, too. I wish I could have been different for you." Helpless, she took another step toward the driveway. She didn't know how to thank him. He could be treating her a lot worse right now, and she would deserve it. "Goodbye, Justin."

"I suppose you need a job?"

"I'll figure out something." Need a job? No, she was frantic for one. How did she tell him the truth?

Find out in
THE RANCHER'S PROMISE
Available June 2010 from Love Inspired

Bestselling author

JILLIAN HART

brings you another heartwarming story
from

the
**GRANGER
FAMILY
RANCH**

Rancher Justin Granger hasn't seen his high school sweetheart
since she rode out of town with his heart. Now she's back, with
sadness in her eyes, seeking a job as his cook and housekeeper.
He agrees but is determined to avoid her...until he discovers
that her big dream has always been him!

The Rancher's Promise

*Available June
wherever books are sold.*

Love Inspired®

After an accident left big-city girl Samantha Harrison in a wheelchair, she returned to her hometown a changed woman. But Bret Conway, her former fiancé, whose heart she broke, insists she's the same girl he loved. Can he help Samantha believe in a second chance?

Look for

Return to Rosewood

by

Bonnie K. Winn

Available June wherever books are sold.

REQUEST YOUR FREE BOOKS!

2 FREE INSPIRATIONAL NOVELS
PLUS 2
FREE
MYSTERY GIFTS

Love Inspired

HISTORICAL
INSPIRATIONAL HISTORICAL ROMANCE

YES! Please send me 2 FREE Love Inspired® Historical novels and my 2 FREE mystery gifts (gifts are worth about $10). After receiving them, if I don't wish to receive any more books, I can return the shipping statement marked "cancel". If I don't cancel, I will receive 4 brand-new novels every other month and be billed just $4.24 per book in the U.S. or $4.74 per book in Canada. That's a saving of over 20% off the cover price. It's quite a bargain! Shipping and handling is just 50¢ per book in the U.S. and 75¢ per book in Canada.* I understand that accepting the 2 free books and gifts places me under no obligation to buy anything. I can always return a shipment and cancel at any time. Even if I never buy another book, the two free books and gifts are mine to keep forever.

102 IDN E4LC 302 IDN E4LN

Name	(PLEASE PRINT)	
Address		Apt. #
City	State/Prov.	Zip/Postal Code

Signature (if under 18, a parent or guardian must sign)

Mail to Steeple Hill Reader Service:
IN U.S.A.: P.O. Box 1867, Buffalo, NY 14240-1867
IN CANADA: P.O. Box 609, Fort Erie, Ontario L2A 5X3
Not valid for current subscribers to Love Inspired Historical books.

Want to try two free books from another series?
Call 1-800-873-8635 or visit www.morefreebooks.com.

* Terms and prices subject to change without notice. Prices do not include applicable taxes. Sales tax applicable in N.Y. Canadian residents will be charged applicable provincial taxes and GST. Offer not valid in Quebec. This offer is limited to one order per household. All orders subject to approval. Credit or debit balances in a customer's account(s) may be offset by any other outstanding balance owed by or to the customer. Please allow 4 to 6 weeks for delivery. Offer available while quantities last.

Your Privacy: Steeple Hill Books is committed to protecting your privacy. Our Privacy Policy is available online at www.SteepleHill.com or upon request from the Reader Service. From time to time we make our lists of customers available to reputable third parties who may have a product or service of interest to you. If you would prefer we not share your name and address, please check here. ☐

Help us get it right—We strive for accurate, respectful and relevant communications. To clarify or modify your communication preferences, visit us at www.ReaderService.com/consumerschoice.

LIH10

Love Inspired. HISTORICAL

TITLES AVAILABLE NEXT MONTH

Available June 8, 2010

THE DOCTOR'S NEWFOUND FAMILY
Valerie Hansen

ROCKY MOUNTAIN MATCH
Pamela Nissen

LIHCNMBPA0510